The
Keeping
Room

ALSO BY ANNA MYERS

Red-Dirt Jessie
Rosie's Tiger
Graveyard Girl
Fire in the Hills
Spotting the Leopard

Anna Myers

The

Keeping

Room

Walker and Company
New York

First published in the United States of America in 1997 by Walker
Publishing Company, Inc.

Published simultaneously in Canada by Thomas Allen & Son Canada,
Limited, Markham, Ontario

Library of Congress Cataloging-in-Publication Data
Myers, Anna.
The keeping room / Anna Myers.
p.   cm.
Summary: Left in charge of the family by his father, who joins the
Revolutionary War effort, thirteen-year-old Joey undergoes such great
changes that he fears he may be betraying his beloved parent.
ISBN 0-8027-8641-3 (hardcover)
1. United States—History—Revolution, 1775–1783—Juvenile fiction.
[1. United States—History—Revolution, 1775–1783—Fiction.
2. Fathers and sons—Fiction.] I. Title.
PZ7.M9718Ke   1997
[Fic]—dc21   97-2964
CIP   AC

Book design by Jennifer Ann Daddio

Printed in the United States of America

2   4   6   8   10   9   7   5   3   1

For my sisters, Linnie Hoover Howell and Shirley Hoover Biggers, who were once my protectors and guides and who became my friends, infinitely precious.

On a hill above the Mountain Fork
you are three,
your ancestors holding strong between you
in a row as straight as a mountain pine.
You are three,
you and your sisters, a patchwork
quilt stitched together by pine needles
and memories your mother gathered
beneath the trees.

—PAUL MYERS

Acknowledgments

A special thank-you goes to my niece, Amy Biggers Trent, who first suggested that I write about Camden and who helped with the research. Thank you also to Amy's husband, Dr. Robert Trent, who gave me excellent medical care when I became ill while visiting.

My brother-in-law, Dr. Charles Biggers, has always helped me. In the early days, he put my manuscripts on his computer. For this book, he drove my sister and me on the research journey, took rolls and rolls of film, and made it possible for me to fly home at once when that suddenly became necessary. Thank you, Charlie.

I am grateful to Agnes Corbett, Director of the Camden Archives and Museum, for her invaluable research assistance.

I owe a great debt to my new friend Ruth Reddick, who showed us through Historic Camden. She went far beyond the call of duty, later writing for me a beautiful description of the things that make her love Camden.

I appreciate the people of Camden for their dedication to the preservation of history that made it possible for me to stand in Kershaw-Cornwallis House and imagine life there during the Revolution. I hope young Joseph and his family would approve of what I imagined and would forgive me the slight liberties I took with what we know of their history.

Chapter One

My father's troops wait on their horses just outside our front door. I can hear the murmuring voices of the men and the snorts and pawings of their mounts, anxious to be down the road to meet the enemy.

"You can't go, Joseph," my mother says, and she makes a wide movement with her arm to indicate the stairway in the front hall of our new home. "There is no railing to hold to." She takes my father's hand and leads him to the stairs. "Will you not stay long enough to see to a railing?"

"My dear," he begins, but my mother pulls away, drops to the second stair, and begins to cry. "Let the house girls walk up and down with the small ones," my father says, but my mother's tears do not stop. "I must go." He bends and kisses her on the top of the head. She does not look up.

My mother cries, I know, not because of the stairs,

but because she is afraid. I want to comfort her, but there is no time.

My father's boots sound loud on the polished planks of our fine oak floors. He is going away. I trot behind him as he crosses the wide hall and catch him just at the door. We step together into the sunlight.

I think perhaps he has not noticed me beside him. I put out my hand to touch his coat sleeve, but I do not. Instead I bite at my lip to hold back the questions I long to hurl his way, questions about his return, about what might lie ahead if he meets the enemy, and most of all about how a frightened boy might borrow of his father's courage.

He is, to my relief, aware of my presence. Just before he begins the long stride down the porch steps, he stops, puts his hand on my shoulder, and speaks. "Stand tall, my boy," he says to me. I shield my eyes because looking up at him means staring into the sun. "Remember all I have taught you. Be brave and strong. There will be ways you can help the men of the town fight should it fall out that my men and I do not stop the bloody British."

For one long moment, he looks only at me. He turns, then, to face his men. "Gentlemen," he calls, "meet my son."

I take one step forward and make a sweeping bow. "He is left to guard the family and our home," my father says. They clap. There are whoops of approval. I am embarrassed, red of face, but I am also proud.

My father glances once more, briefly, into my eyes. I have no wish to say good-bye, but he seems to expect something from me, so I whisper, "I swear, Father, to do just as you have told me." He nods. Then he is gone. Only the pounding of the horses' hooves is left to me. I stand on the great porch, watching the dust settle behind the troops and feeling very small. I rub at my eyes, which have been strained by the brightness of the sun and of my father.

I would like to slip away to the creek, maybe even tramp along through the swamp until I reach the river. Mother would complain that I ruin shoes on such treks, but for a while I could forget about my father having gone to war. I move to the veranda rail and stare toward the water. A great white bird glides above the pine trees. I want to lose myself in the soft dampness of that green world, but my teacher is waiting for me. I turn back into the house and down the stairs to the keeping room.

It is a well-filled larder now, but only days ago, when we were just moving into our new home, the keeping room was empty. Cato supervised the stocking, calling directions to the other slaves. "Rice go here, there go flour, next shelf cornmeal."

George and Sarah, my small brother and sister, dashed about that day sniffing at stores of tea and coffee. "A taste of sugar, please." Sarah pulled at the leg of my trousers. I did not hear at first because I was lost in thought, wondering if the provisions would be for us or the British.

My father has told me the army will be stopped before they reach our town of Camden. I tell myself that my father is always right.

I am, after all, my father's son, named for him, though the third son to be born. My older brothers, James and John, are at school now in England. My mother is glad. "Were they here," she says, "they too would be off to war." I pity my older brothers, forced to live among people who willingly bow to King George.

Both of my older brothers and my younger sisters are like Mother's family, light of skin and hair. Only my little brother and I are not fair, and I am told that Father was pleased at my birth to observe that I appeared more like him. I am like him still with thick dark hair and skin so brown in summer that I might be mistaken for one of the Catawbas, the native tribe that lives in this part of South Carolina.

My brothers early chose professions, James law and John medicine. My father does not seem to mind that they are not interested in his businesses. Since I will take my father's place, I am often at his side as he runs those enterprises. Such activity pleases me. It pleases me too that I am educated at home.

Because my mother's people are Quakers, she has chosen Euven Wylie, also of that faith, as my teacher. Once I thought Euven quite wise, though he is still a young man. I no longer feel so. Euven says there should be no war with England. He says if we Americans would but be patient, we would, in the years to come, outgrow the mother country and become a nation without a fight. My father scoffs at Euven's ideas.

"The soldiers are gone, are they?" Euven is at the great keeping room table. He does not look up at me. His eyes are fixed upon the piece of wood that he is carving. "'Tis foolish for men to kill one another." He stops whittling at the pine he is transforming into Jesus and the little children called unto Him. Euven touches the head of the wooden figure. "Death comes soon enough to us all."

I am disgusted with Euven because his religion has made him weak. "Why do you imagine our Lord looked so?" I question, and I point to his carving. "You have never seen Him, I'll wager."

I would like a good argument, but Euven only smiles. I flop into a chair and open a book, but the lessons do not penetrate my brain. I imagine that I am composing a letter. Dear Father, I am afraid. Have you ever been afraid? Tell me how to make my heart stop pounding.

Suddenly I am aware of Euven's voice. "Thee might

find solace in the writing down of thy thoughts, perhaps in a letter to thy father."

I stare at him. This has happened before, this seeming reading of my mind, and I find it irritating. "There would be no way to send a letter to my father," I say, and I flip the pages of my book.

"Thee could be most honest in a letter never meant to be sent, could thee not?" Euven smiles. "It must not be an easy thing for thee, being the son of a great man."

Father has been gone six days now. A hush hangs over our home as we go quietly about our daily duties. My mother struggles to be brave. She is often at prayer or in conversation with Biddy, the slave who is also her friend.

"We must honor your father with our bravery," she says, and there have been no more visible tears since the day of his departure. Yet I've heard her crying at night.

My sister Mary no longer plays the pianoforte, which Father gave to her upon her last birthday. Even George and Sarah, who are but five and three years of age, seem to have some understanding of what is happening. They do not run and laugh as usual. Only baby Rebecca is completely spared and goes waddling about the nursery with the thick rolls of soft cotton we call her pudding around her waist and head so that she is protected from falls.

If only we could all have a pudding.

Chapter Two

Dear Father,

I went to town this morning. Everywhere there was talk of what the British did to Enoch Groves. Do you remember him, the nephew of Mr. James Groves? He came into our store a few times when he visited his uncle. For a time I listened to the talk in town, but then I had to run away. I ran until no one could see me. At Mr. Giles's garden I stopped. There among the cornstalks I threw up. I am not brave. I am not strong.

⭐ Battle news filters back to us slowly, but our hopes grow weaker each day. There can be little doubt that despite the efforts of my father and his militia the redcoats will come to our home here in Camden, South Carolina. Our town was named for Lord Camden, who Father says tried to befriend us colonists by arguing in Parliament against their right to tax us without representation. The arguments did not work, and now we are colonists no more. We have declared ourselves free, but we must fight the British to prove our point.

I join Mary in the third-floor ballroom. Like the stairs, it is unfinished and the smell of raw pine fills the room. Before Father left, Mary would glide across the floor unmindful of the roughness of the boards beneath her feet and prattle about future balls and the dresses she would wear to them. Now she sits woefully in the middle of the floor.

"Will we ever have dances here, Joey?" she asks when I enter the room.

Mary is but ten, and I am nearer thirteen than twelve. It is my place to ease her mind, but no words come.

I am glad I have not told Mary about poor Enoch Groves. The ballroom has big windows that make it possible to see for a great distance. I am drawn there often to watch for the enemy. I stand there now, once more grateful because I see only the green of pine and poplar, no sign of the horrible red uniforms worn by the British. Still, I can imagine that I hear the notes of their fifes and the pounding of their drums. I shake my head, trying not to think of Enoch Groves.

The English soldiers know no mercy; the king's henchmen, my father calls them. Even without closing my eyes I can see Enoch, just sixteen, barely old enough to go with the patriots in their unsuccessful attempt to defend the city of Charleston. Enoch was captured by the British, but they paroled him.

Just last week a group of redcoats rode by the Groves place over toward Charleston. Enoch was accused of having escaped from the British. He pleaded for his life and showed the soldiers his papers of parole, but neither begging nor papers made a difference.

They killed him in full view of his mother and took him back to their camp. His body was drawn and quartered and stuck up on pikes by the roadside, a British warning to other patriots.

As I stand at the window, it is as if Enoch is there before my eyes. I see the blond hair streaked with blood, and I shudder. A hand touches my arm, and startled, I jump. But it is only my sister. "Joey," she says, "I was talking to you." She pauses and looks closely at my face. "Are you ill?"

I think that if I open my mouth, I may throw up again, or perhaps I will scream. With my lips pressed together, I shake my head.

Mary is still looking at me. "Don't worry, Joey, Father will stop the British. Father will never allow harm to come our way."

I swallow hard and am finally able to speak. "We'll have dancing on the day Father comes home." I wave my arm to include the entire third floor. "Finished or no, there will be a ball here with fiddle music and laughing."

Mary twirls away from me, but I remain by the window. My ears do not hear the laughter or the music of the future ball I have promised Mary. In my mind ring the sobs of Enoch Groves's mother and the chilling sound of British feet keeping time to the drum as they march toward us.

From the third floor hallway come the chimes of the grandfather clock, and I realize it is the appointed hour for lessons. Perhaps studying will make me forget Enoch for a time, yet it does seem foolhardy to continue with Latin and numbers when the enemy is all but at our door.

Euven does not share my opinion. He waits for me in my bedroom with a book already open on my desk.

"I can't settle my mind on studies today," I announce as soon as I have stepped inside. "My father . . ." My words trail off because Euven is shaking his head.

"Thy father," he says, "has issued me wages in advance and told me thy lessons were to continue. What chores I have been paid for I will perform." Euven's legs are long and his arms are strong. True, he deplores violence, but still, I know he would chase me down and carry me back to my books were I to flee.

I stare into his eyes and notice that they are a cloudy blue. I can not see through them into his soul. I wonder about this man who clings to the belief that men must live peacefully together. My mother's family came to this land as Quakers, just as Euven's family did, yet my Uncle Samuel Mathis took up arms against the British.

"Would you refuse to fight, Euven, even if the British came here to kill us all?"

Euven is never in a hurry to speak. He looks at me for a moment, and he smiles. "Only boys say for sure what it is they will do in advance of a crisis. A man knows how hard it is to predict anyone's actions, especially his own."

He motions for me to come take a seat, but I keep my hand on the door. "Might we study again in the keeping room?" I ask.

"And why there?" Euven wants to know, but he begins to gather the books.

"It is my favorite room." I turn and head toward the stairs. I like the keeping room partly because of the smell. In the air the spices, teas, and coffee mix with the rum, which my father uses only for special occasions, such as the drink with his officers before their departure.

Thoughts of the rum cause me pain, because it will

be opened no more until my father's return. How long will the great wooden barrel stand waiting on the corner table?

Walking down the stairs with Euven behind me, I find myself again thinking about Enoch Groves. I try to block the thought from my mind, but I cannot keep from wondering how long before Enoch's head has become only bone? Will the British then take it down, or will they leave him there staring with empty eyesockets?

We settle ourselves at the table where Cato and the other house slaves have their meals. Biddy is busy at the worktable kneading bread. Her new helper is with her. They are both small in stature and step lightly. They will not disturb our lessons. Euven, however, is careful to greet them each, using even the helper's name, Tilda, which I had not known.

Euven, because of his Quaker ways, does not believe in the holding of slaves, and he treats them always as equals. My father says religion can do strange things to a man, but he does see that each baby born into our family is baptized. Then, too, it was he who gave land to the Presbyterians to build their church here, and he says he will gladly give to any faith that desires to establish a church in Camden. I hope God remembers my father's generosity when the battle comes.

"Today," says Euven, "we will read a Greek play

called *Antigone*." I am glad for a break from Latin and numbers, which took all of yesterday's lesson time. At first I enjoy the story of the girl who determines to bury the body of her brother even though she faces grave danger by doing so. "It is the dead, not the living, who make the longest demands," she says.

Suddenly I find the words hard to follow. Even though I am able to read when it is my turn, my mind turns again to Enoch Groves. Might his sister, or perhaps a brother, sneak out to remove his body from the horrible display arranged by the British? Would I have the courage to do such a thing? I am glad Enoch is not my brother, but rather just a boy I've seen a few times.

Enoch's body can make no claim on me, and I shake my head to clear it of all such thoughts. When we have finished with our studies, Tilda brings us a plate of hot scones, dripping with butter, and a pot of tea. I am surprised when Euven forgets the lesson and begins to talk to me as if I am his friend.

"I am musing on the subject of marriage, young Joseph," he says, and he studies his cup of tea closely as he stirs it with his spoon.

I am pleased to be taken so into his confidence. "You think to be married soon?" When he nods, I lean across the table with another question. "What lady?" I ask, and my mind races through the young Quaker ladies of my acquaintance.

"Hannah Goodnight, her father was the tanner who died last year." Euven's voice has music in it when he says her name.

I have seen Miss Hannah Goodnight, have often watched her move about my father's store filling the wicker basket on her arm. I am not too young to have found her comely. Once a comb slipped from the back of her golden hair and fell into a pile of potatoes at my feet. So powerful is the beauty of Miss Hannah Goodnight that it caused my very insides to tremble as I held the comb out to her.

For a moment, I intend to comment to Euven on the pleasure his intended bride brings to the eye, but then I take a piece of Euven's own way and think before I speak. Likely, such a comment would not be seemly coming from me. "I wish you well," I say, and I hold out my hand to shake Euven's just as my father would have done.

"Thy father has paid me well in advance," says Euven. "I'll teach thee for yet another year, and then if God wills it so, I'll take my wife and head west. It's new country I long to see, as new as this country was when the first white man saw it."

The last portion of Euven's speech holds no interest for me. I hear only the part about how my father has paid him one year in advance. Why has my father done this? Is there a possibility that Father will be so long as a year away from home? It is May and the keeping room is warm because of the coals Biddy keeps always burning here on the great stone hearth, but still I shiver.

Chapter Three

Dear Father,

It is hard to fill my days without you. When I walk about in town, men no longer bow their greeting. In fact, I often receive no notice at all. Am I not worthy of a greeting without you? If I am not the son at your side, who can I be?

Mother still calls us all to morning meal together, but the empty chair at the head of the table makes it difficult for us to swallow down our porridge and sausages.

After Jurrusica, the nursery girl, comes for Sarah and baby Rebecca, Mary will busy herself with needlework while Mother goes into the parlor with George to do lessons. Next year George will be taught by Euven as I am. Mary's studies stopped after she learned to read and write. My father does not think it important to educate girls. Mary does not agree. I know she has taken my books from time to time, but I have never discussed any bit of learning with my sister. It is my place to hold the same ideas as my father.

There is nothing worthy to occupy my time. I am accustomed to spending mornings following my father about his holdings. The store was always interesting with its shoppers and clerks who hurry to dust shelves, pretending they do not see my father step, tall and straight, through the door.

We used to go also to Father's two mills, one a gristmill grinding flour and one a sawmill for turning timbers into building materials. Because it was his first business, the gristmill is most dear to my father. Before he went away, we would stand, he and I, for long periods of time beside the great millstones and watch them grind grain between them. Father's voice would mix with the splashing sounds of water against the vast wheel. Always his story was the same.

"I built this mill with my own two hands, Joey, owned no slaves yet then, did I." The mill on Pine Tree Creek has been good to my father. "In a span of but five years, boy," he would say, "my holdings in this backcountry grew to include the sawmill, indigo works, tobacco warehouse, the brewery, and large mercantile businesses here at Camden and at Cheraw."

"And lands," I would put in. "Don't forget your lands."

"That's right, son," he would say. "All in but five years, and I was ready then to ask for your mother's hand." Never tiring of the story, I would stand beside my father and listen. Even in winter when the air from off the mill pond was near ice, I felt warm.

The troubles with England were never far from my father's thoughts, and on our mornings together he often talked to me of what boiled within him. I remember a day, not a month past, though it seems much longer ago, when Father said to me, "They'd have us in chains, son, making laws for us without giving us any say." He removed the arm that rested around my shoulder and, forming a fist, he raised it to the sky. "I did not come to this country to become a slave," he shouted.

It would not have surprised me to have learned that King George himself heard my father's words, but then, of course, had my father's message carried across the sea, the king on his throne would have called a halt to the war. Not even a king, I believed, would have the nerve to ignore my father's warnings.

Later that day when we left the mill and went home

for our midday meal, Father's words about being a slave came again to my mind as Cato ran from the keeping room's front doors to lift to his small shoulders the large bag my father had carried from the store.

"Father," I whispered, "do you suppose Cato and the others wanted to leave Africa and become slaves?"

My father frowns. I know he and my mother do not agree about how slaves should be treated. I have heard him say, "It is not seemly for you to be so friendly with the cook, my dear."

He stopped and placed his hand on my shoulder, looking into my eyes as he spoke. "Do not trouble yourself about such things, Joey. Slavery fits the order of things. Without slaves, who would tend the rice on Carolina's plantations?"

I nodded. He smiled, and I trotted so as to stay up with my father as he climbed the great steps that would lead us to dine at our well-laid table.

Now, with my father gone, I spend my mornings wandering about in the swamp that lies not far behind our house. There I climb through the hanging moss of a live oak tree and settle upon a strong limb. I sit absolutely still, watching for a blue heron and listening to the cry of the other birds.

I wonder where my father is. It comes to my mind that he may be dead, but then I dismiss the thought. Are not the yellow warbler and the little brown wren still holding forth with their morning songs? Surely, no bird in all of South Carolina would call out joyously if Colonel Kershaw were no more.

But on this particular day in late May of 1780, I do not dress for a day in the swamp. Instead I put on a new linen shirt with ruffles at the throat and sleeves to show from beneath my waist coat. I also choose a pair of my best silk stockings to fasten with garters at my knee breeches. I am going to town, and the son of Colonel Kershaw must cut a fine figure on the streets of Camden. But a thought comes to me, and I say aloud, "He must also put on start-ups." So I pull the large boots over my buckled shoes to protect them from the mud in the streets of our little city.

"Camden needs boardwalks, Joseph." I remember my mother scolding my father at our evening meal one day last spring. "I might find it pleasing to go about town except for all that mud. Don't you think you ought to see to the walks?"

"Send Cato to town, my dear. Do you forget that you are the wife of Camden's founder and most prosperous citizen? And perhaps you forget that we are at war. I have the redcoat enemies to see to." He pushed his chair back from the table.

"I do not forget the war," Mother said and her voice took on a sad sound, "but in truth I would like to."

Then immediately she began to urge each of us children to take more smoked ham from the big platter.

Now, as I dress to go about town, I know that even had I not covered my shoes, I too would be more worried about the redcoats than about the mud. I try to set my cocked hat at an angle that will make me look jaunty and unafraid.

I do not tell Mother that I am going. I cannot bear to see the questions in her eyes, so I slip quietly down the stairs. From the open parlor door, I hear her discussing George's copy book with him. "Too many ink blobs," she complains. "You must be more careful with your quill."

Our new house is built on a small hill slightly away from the rest of the town. I stand on the high porch and look down on what once seemed a safe, peaceful world. Before me lies our green, thick and undisturbed now except by the occasional cow or horse that Cato might stake there to graze. Once the green vibrated with the sound of balls being whacked with cricket bats and with the sound of boys' excited voices. There was a time, even before the new house was built, when we played there almost every day after our evening meal.

There has been no game since last October. Jacob, the blacksmith's son, had time away from his father's shop that last game day. We laughed in the autumn sun, pushing one another good naturedly. But things went bad when David Brinker lost his temper with Charlie Eaton. "It's not your turn, Tory," he shouted.

"It is." Charlie raised his fists, ready to strike. "And I'd rather be a Tory than rotten no-good rabble."

The game was over. I knew it was Charlie's turn, and I knew that Charlie had a friendlier spirit than David Brinker, who whined when he lost a game. Still, the sides were drawn, and I stood with the other boys whose fathers were ready to fight the king.

Only Lynn Noll stood with Charlie as a loyalist. I liked both boys and wanted just to go on with the cricket game. Instead I grabbed up a small stick and threw it at Charlie. "Give this to your king," I shouted.

We drove them running from the field. There has not been another game since that day. Tory families have mostly left town by now. Jacob has no time at all away from the shop now that his older brother has gone to fight. I used to love to play cricket. I cross the green quickly, tromping the damp grass beneath my feet.

When I head west on Wateree Street, which is named for the nearby river, I am forced to walk in the road. The sand has changed to mud that sucks at my start-ups and slows my progress. At Meeting Street I turn, planning to stop first at Thompson's blacksmith shop. Jacob likely will be busy at the forge, heating iron

until it is soft, or he may be pounding at the anvil until
the iron becomes a horseshoe or a cooking utensil.

There will be no chance for a real visit with Jacob,
but men frequently stand about watching the work.
Once they gathered too at our house discussing the war
with my father. I miss their deep tones and the smell of
their pipe tobacco, but even more I hunger after news.

But as I grow near the shop, I hear no voices, no
hammering. The big doors are open, but I see that the
fire at the great forge is little more than coals. Wondering, I dash through the shop to the dwelling entrance
at the back. I knock loudly, but there is no answer.
Mistress Thompson and the younger children are gone
too.

Leaving the dim shop and moving back into the
sunlight, I shade my eyes and look down the empty
street. Where are the people? Have the British come
and carted them all away? The innkeeper's wife hurries
from her front door, which is in the middle of the
block. "Where is everyone?" I yell.

She is moving away from me as quickly as her short,
plump legs will carry her, and I strain to catch her shout
of "Square."

The town square, of course! Something has happened and everyone is gathered at the square. I feel re-
sentful that no one has come to Kershaw House to tell

us, but my resentment does not keep me from moving. Unlike the mistress of the inn, I do not stick to the street. Instead I dart between the houses and shops, making a more direct path to the square. My start-ups slow my pace, and I toss them aside. The shoes, I think, may go too. If necessary I will not hesitate to run through the town in my silk stockings.

Behind one house my way is blocked by a large pig-pen. I hurdle the fence, ignoring the snorts of the pigs. At the other side, I jump again. This time my hat falls from my head. I do not look back at it. Let the pigs quarrel over which of them might look best in a cocked hat.

The crowd I see as I come out on Broad Street is big. Men in their work clothes, some with tools still in hand, women with the lace caps they wear only inside still upon their heads, and children everywhere. Even old Grandfather Murphy, who must have been carried, sits under a tree.

My exhaustion forces me to slow at the back of the crowd. But, breathing heavily, I begin to shove my way forward, because someone shouts, "We've gathered now. Out with it."

As I push between two ladies, one of them swats at me with the end of her long apron and says, "Mind your manners there, young fellow." Ignoring her, I drop down to crawl between the widespread legs of a tall man in leather breeches. I listen while I move, catching comments that tell me battle news has just arrived. Now my heart beats fast as much from fear as from running.

Isaac Kent, who owns the tavern, seems to be acting as town leader in my father's absence. He holds up a hand to the crowd. "Let all be silent," he calls. "We will hear the boy now."

Just a space or two away from Mr. Kent, near a large wooden barrel, stands a boy. He looks to be perhaps two years younger than I am. His clothing is like that of a farmer, with worn shirt and no stockings showing between the coarse woolen breeches and broken shoes. Mr. Kent gives a leg up to the boy who climbs upon the barrel and removes his broad felt hat.

The crowd still murmurs. "Silence!" the tavern owner thunders. "Let Will have his say."

The boy wipes his hands first across his face and then upon his breeches legs, and with a deep breath he begins. "Forty miles or so from here it be. Not two miles from me own home, out in the open woods, just trees by and by, not so as for cover. It fell out this way. Tarleton was the British commander, and a fellow named Buford leading our side. Them that lived told it, some with their last breaths. Tarleton sounded his bugle."

Will holds an imaginary horn up to his lips, but the

crowd moaned. "Go on, lad," urged Mr. Kent. "Leave off the bugling."

The boy looks disappointed but continues his story. "Tarleton advanced with the infantry in the center and the cavalry to the sides. Buford's rear guard got hit first." Will's eyes appear to be almost popping from his head. "Cut to pieces they was. Lieutenant Pearson was shot down, then got his nose cut off and his lips too. Even his eyes knocked out, but he was still a-breathing when I rode off." He pauses to take a breath.

"For God's sake, lad, what happened to Buford's other men? Did they hold firm?" someone shouts.

"Stood their ground they did at first, but when they discovered the cavalry a-coming round to the rear, Buford gave the order to drop arms and surrender. Cruit, him what hoisted the flag of truce, was cut down. Them redcoats took to massacring, tossing wounded about on their bayonets and torturing them to death. Blood running everywhere and all the begging for mercy going for nothing."

Except for some gasps the crowd stays amazingly quiet. I cannot bear to focus on what he is saying. Instead I stare at his legs, bare and red from being held close to the horse on the long ride.

Then I force myself to look about me, knowing that behind those white faces minds grope with the same question burning in my own. I wait for someone to shout, "Colonel Kershaw's Camden troops, were they with Buford's slaughtered men?"

As if by some silent pledge, no one asks the question and Will goes on. "Tarleton took prisoners, not so many. Dead and dying was everywhere. More than a hundred dead, me pa wagers. He's there now along with others, helping the Reverend Carnes put bodies in one big grave and toting them what might live over to Waxhaw Church to be treated. 'Ride quick to Camden,' me pa says to me. 'Carry the news.'"

I am my father's son, I tell myself. It is I who must give voice to the question. "The Camden men," I yell, "led by Colonel Kershaw? Were they in the battle?"

Not a stir moves through the crowd. Will's face twists. He has not thought, it seems, about to whom he speaks. His answer, little more than a whisper, vibrates through my ears and out into the mud of the street. "Fought bravely, they did."

The crowd breaks loose then. "My boy, Jim Wheeler, do you know his fate?"

"Roger Watts, a tall man, what of him?"

"Did you see Robert James?"

"My husband," screams a young woman with a babe in her arms. "Scott's his name?"

Will's head drops, his chin upon his chest. There is no joy in the telling now. "I don't know no names," he says. "Not none at all." Scrabbling down with his gaze lowered, he runs across the square and retreats into the safe darkness of the tavern's open door.

A few people go after him, but most of the crowd makes no move to follow him or to break up. Instead they huddle in small groups talking in soft voices. The sound of weeping comes from some of them.

I stand miserably alone, staring down at my mud-covered breeches, stockings, and shoes. I want to think about my ruined clothing. I do not want to think of the massacre. I do not want to let the pictures form in my mind, pictures of my father's body, broken and bleeding.

Move, I tell myself. Moving is better. Without making a real decision to go there I start toward the tavern door, mud sucking at my shoes. My father, well known in the area, would likely have been recognized. I can find Will, demand to know what he could tell me of the fate of Colonel Kershaw.

Just inside the tavern door, I pause, waiting for my eyes to become accustomed to the dim light. I see Will in the far corner, his back pushed against the wall.

Someone has brought him a mug along with bread and a strip of some kind of meat. For a moment I watch as he tears at the meat and bread, then takes a swig from the mug.

"I done told. I can't call a single name." He pushes against the wall with his back as if he hopes to go through and be outside away from the questions about to come.

I want to move closer to him, but my feet refuse to be lifted. "Joseph Kershaw, Colonel Joseph Kershaw? I daresay you know that name?" I am pleased because I think my voice is steady and loud, like that of a man.

"I don't. Just let me be," he whimpers, and I think he is about to cry. I also think he lies. I will go to him, jerk him up by the front of his dirty shirt, and beat him into the wall. He is a coward, and I can make him talk.

My feet remain planted just inside the doorway. It is you who is the coward, I accuse myself inside my head. You are afraid to know the truth of your father's fate. I turn and run from the accurate voice of accusation.

Outside people are still standing about. I see Isaac Kent with Blacksmith Thompson, the innkeeper, baker, and the Presbyterian minister. I go to them and listen. Very aware that as a mere boy I should not speak until I am spoken to, I remain quiet. But the gist of the conversation begins to come to me, and I am amazed.

"We're agreed, then?" Isaac Kent is a small man, but he pulls himself up straight and stares squarely into the face of each man in the group.

"There's nothing else for it. Nothing but to meet them with surrender," says Mr. Thompson.

"No," screams from my throat. Amazed, the men

turn to look at me, but I rush on. "We have powder in the magazine." I point wildly in the direction of my home and the nearby brick structure where ammunition is stored.

"Hush, boy," says Mr. Kent.

"Kershaw has spoiled the lad," says the baker, and he shoots a snarl in my direction.

Only Reverend Fielding looks at me kindly. "The boy deserves an explanation. His father has strived valiantly to defend us." He comes to stand near me and places his hand on my shoulder. "The powder is even now being loaded so that it can be taken to Charlotte. 'Tis better than letting it fall into enemy hands." He shakes his head and his face is sad. "There's no hope for us, young Joseph, not against so many."

"Good Lord, boy, did you not hear what happened at the battle?" Mr. Kent turns away from me, and the others do the same.

Wretched, I begin to step backward, away from them. My entire body is shaking as if it were but a tree branch in a violent windstorm.

"My wife can make the truce flag." The minister's words come to my ear. I whirl and flee across the green, through the muddy streets, and up the hill toward my home.

I can imagine my mother, sitting in the parlor. By now it is her time to read aloud to George and Sarah.

Perhaps baby Rebecca toddles about in her pudding. Who will protect them?

At the edge of town, I am forced to rest for a moment, and I lean against the trunk of a dead pine tree.

"Cut off his nose and lips." The words slip from my own mouth, but so unlike my voice is the sound that at first I want to look behind me for the speaker. I am alone, of course, and feeling more afraid than I had ever imagined possible. I take one long, slow breath, and then I run again. I move across our green with no thoughts of cricket. My legs threaten to buckle beneath me, but I run still, up the grassy knoll toward the home of my father, Joseph Kershaw, whose body may at this moment lie in a mass grave out near the old Salisbury Road.

Chapter Four

Dear Father,

*Where are you? I know about the terrible battle. You aren't
dead. You can't be dead. Were you afraid during the
battle? I would have been so afraid. The British are
coming our way. No one wants to fight them. Even Mother
says we must make our peace with them. How can I do
that? I am your son. I cannot surrender to the British. I do
not know what to do.*

I stand now at the window. Staring out I see
Cato, a hoe resting against his shoulder, heading
toward the vegetable garden. Is it possible that life in
this house will go on just as before while we wait for
the British to come?

When I told Mother the news, she sat quietly for a

while. "We will do whatever we must do to live," she said. Her face was white with fear, but she stood. "I must go over menus with Biddy."

Mother walked toward the door, but she looked back at me and smiled. "It is sometimes just as brave to know when not to fight as it is to fight."

Just as always, Euven comes for studies. "I've been paid to do lessons, not stand about in the streets talking of war as do most of the people in town," he says when he arrives. "Speculation will do no good at this point." He takes books from his knapsack and places them upon the keeping room table. On top is a geometry book. We have only recently begun the study.

"Pythagorean Theorem," he says with pleasure, and he touches the book cover gently.

I look at this person and think it is a waste, a man whose tall, muscular frame all but fills the doorway to a room, a man who can fell a deer with his musket at a distance before other men have even observed the animal. I shake my head. What a pity that such a man is a Quaker and a teacher when he could be with our fighting men, could be, even at his young age, a leader among them.

I do not share Euven's enthusiasm for our new subject, and even on a good day my mind would be apt to wander. Through the window near our table, I can see Jurrusica in the back garden with George and Sarah.

Laughing, George runs after a hoop. Sarah struggles with a pair of stilts. She falls, her white underpetticoat flapping in the wind, but getting up at once, she tries again. The garden is full of red and yellow flowers in bloom.

I jump up. "I must do something," I shout. "I can't just sit and wait for the murderers to come to our door."

Euven reaches for my arm and draws me back down to my chair. "This is a nice room." He waves at the shelves. "Thy favorite room, I believe thee said." He pauses and he smiles at me. "Thee must have a keeping room inside thyself, young Joseph, a place to store what is good, what will make thee strong when thee most need strength."

I slump miserably, my face in my hands. "What can I have inside? I do not know what Father would have me do."

"Then," says Euven, "perhaps it is time thee begin to think for thyself."

"But I believe my father lives," I say. "If he were dead, something would tell me. I would know, do you not agree?"

He does not answer at once. Rising, he paces toward the great hearth. "I agree that hope is good," Euven says at last, and his eyes are full of sympathy. "There will be time for mourning, when there is no hope. But I believe thee must learn to keep thy own counsel."

"While my father lives, I must try to do what he would bid me." I write *Joseph Kershaw* upon my slate. It is not my name I spell. It is that of my father. It is not the name of my late father.

Somehow Euven gets me through the lessons. When he leaves, I stay in the keeping room, staring at the coals on the hearth. Finally night comes, but sleep does not come with it. I lie watching the moonlight play upon the heavy curtain. Across the hall, my mother moves about her room. When I hear her go out into the hallway, I rise and join her.

"You should go back to bed, Joey," she says, but she does not insist. Instead she takes a place on the hall settee and pats the spot beside her.

When I am settled, I decide to try my theory on Mother. "I believe Father lives." I clear my throat and go on. "If he were dead, I would feel his death inside."

My mother nods, and she smiles. "I have thought the same thing. Yes, he lives. He must live." She reaches for my hand. "You are a man, Joey, perhaps not in years, but you are a man now."

With a shake of the head I disagree. "Not man enough to protect this family. Mother, perhaps we could go to Burndale, be with Uncle Samuel."

"There will be no fleeing the British. If they come here, they will go too to Burndale. Have you forgotten your Uncle Samuel is already a British prisoner of war on parole?"

It is true, I suppose. My uncle will surely be watched by the enemy. He has been captured by them once and allowed to return to Burndale, but they will keep an eye on him if they come into the area. While Mother talks, my head is turned in her direction. Out of the corner of my eye I see something.

After being sent back to bed, I lie again in the room I share with my little brother. This time, however, I do not stare idly at the curtain. Now I have a mission. Now I have an idea. When enough time has gone by with no sound from my mother's room, I will act.

To pass the interval, I whisper, over and over, my father's words, "Stand tall." When at last Mother is still, I slip from bed, stepping carefully upon the rays of moonlight that dance across the shiny oak floor.

The floors, being new, do not creak. I do not have far to go. Above the hall settee is a rack. On that rack is a pistol. Not able to reach the gun, I climb on the satin cushion.

The gun feels cold in my hands. I stand for a moment striving to quiet my beating heart. I have held this same pistol before when shooting with my father, but I have never held it with such a purpose as I hold it now.

Barely breathing, I go back to my room. Inside I try to decide where I shall hide the gun. I consider my wardrobe, among my clothing, but of course Mother would look there at once.

Standing in my room, my father's pistol in my hands, I look all about my chamber for a place to conceal the weapon. My search brings nothing to mind. When my glance falls on my brother George, I step closer to the bed. In the moonlight I study him, my younger brother so like me, the same high forehead, the same dark hair. George, however, is not a man. At seven he is little more than a baby.

A great desire to protect my brother envelops me, but when my lips move, it is a promise to my father that is produced. "I'll shield him, Father. I swear I'll shield them all."

As the words leave my mouth, an idea comes to me. Perhaps, I think, it is a message sent to me from my father through the night air, just as my promise was sent to him.

I move at once out of my room and toward the stairs. In the darkness I stay close to the wall because of the missing rail, but still I am soon met with the aromas of the keeping room.

Ham lingers from the cooking of our evening meal, spices always, and the comforting smell of earth, which I know clings to the rakes, hoes, and other garden tools stored in the corner. At the bottom of the stairs, I stand savoring the smells and looking about the massive room, the inner workings, the guts of our elegant home.

The doors, just under our front porch, are huge and can open wide so that supply carts are driven inside on the brick floor. At the opposite end is the great fireplace where cooking for the entire household is done. A large woodbox stands beside the vast stone hearth.

It is there I will hide the pistol. Kneeling, I begin to take out each stick of wood, placing it quietly on the floor. When most of the pieces are moved, I place the pistol on the bottom in the center of the large box. Gently I stack the wood over it. When I finish, I sigh and rest my hand on a top log. Now, I have only to make sure the woodbox is always full. Biddy will be glad to have my help. I will tell her Father asked me to see to some chore each day.

Euven has told me to keep a room inside myself for good things that will make me strong. I smile. It will be easier to be strong with a gun hidden in the keeping room.

Rising, I turn to make my way back upstairs, but instead I gasp. There in the shadows against the wall is a figure I had failed to notice. Cato! He lies on a pad such as the lesser slaves use for sleeping. He, who has a much nicer bed elsewhere, has chosen to sleep here on the hard brick floor.

It takes only a second for me to realize why he is here. The keeping room is Cato's realm. It is here that he takes count of our provisions and from here he directs other workers. In my father's absence he thinks it better to sleep on this floor.

Moreover, I am aware that his eyes are now open. I can spot his white hairs among the dark, and I see that his head is raised, resting on a hand with the arm bent at the elbow. Cato has watched me. Cato knows my secret.

I make no movement. I can feel, rather than see, his eyes boring into me. Cato, unlike the other slaves, does not defer to me. When I was small and toddling behind my father at his business, it was often Cato's quick hand that swatted my bottom and pointed me in a different direction if I came near mischief or danger.

Now I wait for him to say something. Will he scold me? Will he demand that I return the pistol to its proper place? For a long minute no words are said, no movement is made. Then Cato lowers his head, and I believe he closes his eyes.

I start for the stairs, but Cato's voice stops me. "Yo' might got the master's gun, boy, but ol' Cato knows who yo' is. Does yo'? Before yo' point that gun at a living thing make sure it's something yo' want dead, cause that's what guns does, boy."

Cato's words anger me. "I am my father's son," I

say. I do not wait for an answer. I put my foot down hard upon the first step, but the sound does not block out Cato's disapproving snort.

When the first light of day comes, I am out of bed and at my window. No sign of the British! Looking down from the slight hill on which our house sits, I see smoke arise from the dwellings in town. Roosters call their greetings to one another. I see a carriage drawn by two horses. A lady and a gentleman sit on the seat. The horses' gait does not speak of hurry. I go to the other window from which I can see more of the town. People move about the streets, but none of them are British soldiers. All is yet well in Camden.

Downstairs I find the door open to the keeping room, and I hear my mother's step on the stairs and her voice calling, "Cato, the pistol is missing from the hall. Cato?"

I follow. If my secret is to be revealed so early on, I must know. Stopping on the last step, I hope to see and hear without being noticed.

Cato stands beside the table where his breakfast of grits and sausage sits half eaten. "No, ma'am. I never touched Master's gun," he said. "I'll search through quarters if you thinks someone there has stole it."

He waits, head bowed slightly, for my mother to speak. I grin, realizing he has kept my secret without actually lying.

"No." My mother sighs and begins to turn away. "Go back to your food. If you didn't take the gun, I expect I've only to look in Joey's chamber."

I back quietly up the stairs a ways and then head down, stepping hard. Of course, Mother hears me.

"Good," she says when I am visible, "I was about to come up to you. What have you done with your father's gun?"

For a moment, I consider lying. Behind Mother I can see Cato at the table. His head is cocked to one side, his eyebrow is raised. Then he points his finger at me. I know that he is warning me to come out with the truth before he does.

"Mother," I plead. "The British are certain to come to our door. Would you have me without a weapon?"

"Yes," she says flatly. She steps toward me and brushes from my eyes the hair I have failed to tie back. "To resist will mean death. Bring the gun to me now."

"I am the man here now, Mother. Did you not say so?" I try to make my voice strong as I repeat, "Did you not say so?"

She nods her head. "You are, but I am still your mother. Bring me the pistol."

"I will keep the pistol," I say, and my gaze meets hers, unflinching.

I expect her to make the demand again and more forcefully, but she only wipes her hand across her eyes.

"I forbid you to use that weapon," she tells me. "And when I find it, I shall take it myself to the woods and bury it until your father's return."

No words come to my mind, so, staring down at the brick floor, I move away from the narrow stairs. Again my mother touches my hair, then goes quickly up the steps. Cato gives me one satisfied smile before turning to give full attention to his sausage and grits.

When Euven comes again in the afternoon, he makes no effort to spread the books upon the keeping room table where I have waited for him. "Perhaps one day skipped will not ruin thy mind," he says. He pauses a moment, then goes on. "Riders bring the message that the British will be here tomorrow. General Cornwallis leads them."

At once I am on my feet. "Will they march by or stay?" I ask and I grip the back of the chair.

Euven shrugs his broad shoulders. "Who can say? It may not be as bad as thee imagine."

"Then I wish they were here now." I hear my voice tremble, and I am barely holding back tears. I drop back into my chair, and slump forward, resting my head and arms upon the table.

Euven leans over to where I sit to touch my shoulder. "Several men have decided to meet the soldiers outside of town with a flag of truce. I think as a Kershaw son, thee would be welcome among them."

I look up at him, and I bite at my lip. "My father says it is better to die a free man than to live a slave to British masters."

"Thy father does not wish thee to die," says Euven.

"I hate the British." I pound my fist against the table.

"Hate is the most powerful of slave masters," Euven says gently. "I wish I could teach thee that, young Joseph. It is a truth harder to learn even than geometry."

"How can I do else but hate them? They are butchers!"

"I cannot but believe good and bad men abound on both sides."

We are quiet for a while. I close my eyes. The keeping room sounds fill my ears. Biddy's soft humming as she peels potatoes at her workbench competes with the sound of water boiling in a huge pot hanging above the fire. I decide to concentrate on the song, a familiar tune the slaves sing about how God delivered the Israelites from Egypt.

Finally, Euven reaches for my arm and pulls. I open my eyes. "Have thee decided? Will thee meet the British with promises of surrender?"

"Will you go with me?"

"I will stand beside thee," he promises.

Chapter Five

Dear Father,

I am to be among the men who surrender our town to the British. Are you disappointed in me? Know that I have not really given up. I have your pistol. A time may yet come for me to strike against them.

The next morning Isaac Kent is in charge of the group of men who meet to walk just outside of town, where they will wait for the coming army.

Euven and I approach the group before they are all gathered, and he tells the others that we wish to join them. Mr. Kent studies me. "This is not the time for crying," he says, "or for any other boyish nonsense."

I nod my head. "Young Joseph Kershaw is more than just a boy," says Euven.

"You will be beside him?" asks the baker.

Euven promises to keep an eye on me, and they agree that we may join them.

No one talks as we move down the street. Yesterday's sun has dried most of the mud to hard lumps of sand. Mostly I keep my eyes on the prints left by the shoes of the men who walk before me.

Just a few feet past the last small dwelling, Isaac Kent raises his arm. "Here," he calls. "Spread in a line across the road." Euven and I end up in the middle of the line, with me beside Reverend Fielding, who holds the flag.

We are quiet, and the sun shines warm upon my head and shoulders. Euven has turned to look back at the little house. "Hannah lives there," he whispers. "With her mother and young brother." I too glance back. There is a face at one of the windows.

Then we catch the first strains of music. Just as I had imagined so many times, we hear them before they come into view. The pounding of their feet and the music of their drums and fifes grow louder and louder as they come.

"They gave no heed to the truce flag in the battle," I murmur to Euven. "Cut him to pieces who held it."

My whisper must have been heard by the minister. He shifts the flag, which was attached to a broomstick, from one hand to the other. "But they were soldiers.

We are civilians. They will not harm us." He speaks loudly to the group in general, then drops his voice. It is unclear whether he now speaks only to himself or to me, but I strain to hear the words. "My Bess made the flag, hemmed it nice."

I study the flag, made from sparkling white material, made large too so that the British could not fail to see. I wondered if the minister thinks the British will be impressed by a well-hemmed flag. But how could I know? Maybe they will be. I say nothing, only try hard to smile at Reverend Fielding, who pats me on the shoulder.

Just then they come in sight at the top of the hill. At first there is only one line, even with a row of small pine trees. The green, however, does not move, while the red comes on and on. Only the minister speaks. "Dear God," he cries.

I stare, mesmerized by the scarlet procession that moves over the hill in the blazing sunlight. On and on they come. I feel certain they will march over our group of men, trampling the carefully made flag beneath their great boots. On they will go until the whole of Camdem is covered by red. The drumbeat drills into my very bone.

Reverend Fielding steps forward with the flag. The broom handle shakes in his hands, but I do not fault him for his fear. I think that I too am shaking, but I am unsure of almost everything except the line of soldiers about to engulf us.

As in a dream nothing seems quite real. A soldier with much gold braid upon his uniform steps forward and takes the flag from Reverend Fielding, who bows slightly and moves quickly back to be among us.

"I accept you all as prisoners of war for His Majesty, King George. You will now answer to the direction of Lord Cornwallis." His words are almost sung, clear and loud enough to carry, I think, across our small town.

For a second I think the soldier is Cornwallis, but just as I realize Lord Cornwallis would not walk, a great white horse comes snorting to the front. The rider sits tall in the saddle. His wig is as white as the horse, and his red coat is more decorated than any of the others.

A bugle blasts and another soldier steps forward. There is a sheet in his hand, and in the same singsong voice as the former one, but not as loud, he begins to read.

"All cattle and other livestock are hereby to be rendered as property of His Majesty's army. All businesses will be run under military direction. The property of one Joseph Kershaw, traitor to the crown, is hereby seized."

The voice goes on, but the words are lost to my ear. Property! They will take the mills, the flour mill and the sawmill, the store, and the house. Our house!

Slowly, hoping not to be noticed, I inch back. When I am behind the line of townsmen, I turn and run.

It is possible, I know, that I will be ordered to halt. I do not even listen. Let them shoot me if they will, but I will run until a musket ball knocks me down. I must warn my mother.

My mind moves as fast as my feet over the grass of the town, past the square where my father drilled his militia men, away from the scattered homes and places of trade, across our green, and up the little hill to home. In my mind's eye I see the British. They shove my mother and treat her like a slave. I see one with his bayonet ready to run through my little brother because he spills a mug of ale he is ordered to carry.

I cannot bear to imagine more, and I shake my head. "Stop these awful thoughts," I scream to myself. "You must think clearly."

Of course, they have been watching. Mother and Cato wait for me on the porch. With my last shred of energy, I thrust myself up the stairs and into my mother's arms. "They're coming here to take our house," I gasp.

My mother pays no heed to my words. Instead she makes soft, soothing sounds and wipes my face with her linen handkerchief. "Be calm, Joey. Be calm. I've expected this. Of course, Cornwallis is coming here." She motions toward town. "Where else do you suppose he would find quarters to his liking? We will be calm, Joey, and face them together." She motions again, and this time I turn and look in the direction she has pointed.

As if I have pulled them behind me, the great line of red moves through the town and up the hill. Within minutes the British army will claim our home as theirs. I move to the porch rail and lean upon it, staring at the red line moving like a snake to shoot its poison into our waiting bodies.

"Bring the other houseworkers," my mother says in a steady voice to Cato, "and the children. I want my children with me."

The others must have been watching through the window in the entry hall because Cato is back with them at once. Jurrusica carries baby Rebecca and leads Sarah by the hand. George holds onto Mary's skirt.

Mother takes the baby in one arm and puts the other around Sarah's shoulder. George runs to me and wraps his arms about my waist. Mary steps determinedly to be next to Mother. There is fire in her eyes. My sister's bravery shames me, and I pull in a deep breath. "Stand tall." I remember Father's words to me, and I make myself as tall as possible.

The servants are gathered behind us. I hear Biddy and Tilda muttering prayers beneath their breaths. "Will they eat us?" asks Sarah.

"Certainly not," says my mother. "Human beings do not eat one another."

I know, of course, that she does not speak the exact truth. I have heard of cannibals, and I have heard of British cruelty. Being eaten might not be the worst thing that befalls us. I bend and lift Sarah into my arms.

Mary reaches back to pat Sarah's leg. "If they eat me," she says, "they shall find me tough indeed." She folds her arms across her chest. "In fact, Lord Cornwallis himself might just break a tooth if he bites into the likes of me." She laughs. Sarah and George have both crossed their arms in imitation of Mary.

The soldiers are on our green now, and I see that there are not as many as marched into town. The others, I am sure, have been assigned business elsewhere. The same officer who spoke earlier steps forward. "By the order of Lord Cornwallis I claim this house as property of King George the Third and declare it to be used as headquarters to Lord Cornwallis and His Majesty's troops."

Mother makes ready by stepping forward as if to say something, but the soldiers pay her no mind. A group of them move up the steps and head for the door. Only by stepping aside do we avoid being knocked down. We huddle there watching until one soldier stops, sticks out his musket, and motions. "Inside," he barks.

Their heavy boots stomp across our polished floors.

Mother drops to her knees and touches one of the great scars cut into the shine. I too stare at the scars and know with a terrible certainty that our lives will be similarly marred.

And so our splendid new home passes from our hands to the hands of the enemy. The soldier who motioned us in pulls at mother's arm. "In there," he says, and he herds our family into the parlor, where we are left with a Captain Harkins. He seems to have been placed in charge of the rebel family, which is what we are called. He is a young soldier, about Euven's age, I think.

The captain speaks in a formal tone, all business, but it seems to me there is a surprising kindness in his eyes. Of course, his kindness makes no difference. He is our jailor. Our home has become our prison. A great hatred burns inside me for Captain Harkins and all other redcoats.

My mother interrupts him as he speaks of how we will be, always, watched. "May we know what has become of my husband, Colonel Kershaw?" she asks coldly. She has refused his offer of a seat and still holds the baby. The rest of us crowd around her.

"He is a prisoner, madam, being brought this day to Camden Jail."

"Injured?" My mother's voice is little more than a whisper.

"No."

"God be praised." She sinks to the sofa. For a moment I think tears of relief will fall, but then she pulls herself together. "What will become of him?"

The Captain looks down briefly at his boots. "He will be given the opportunity to repent of his rebellion and join His Majesty's forces."

It is Mary, standing beside me, who speaks first. "He won't. You can just bet your red coat he won't!" Mother shakes her head in an effort to stop Mary, but my sister stomps her patent leather shoe against the parlor floor.

Captain Harkins stares at Mary, who boldly meets his gaze. A bit of a smile plays about the captain's lips. I think that he admires Mary's determination. He is about to speak when another soldier speaks up.

"Well, then, little miss," says another officer who has just entered the room. "We shall have the pleasure of hanging your loving father." He pauses then and flashes a vile grin at my sister. "And you, my dear, shall have a special place of observation."

"Let me deal with the family, please, Keegan," says Captain Harkins, and he frowns at the other soldier.

"As you wish. As you wish." Keegan turns to walk away, but over his shoulder he adds, "Only why not let them see how it is from the start-off?"

I watch his red form move through the door, and I

repeat his name to myself. I think we shall see Keegan again, and the meeting will not be pleasant.

Sarah and George begin to whimper, and Mary leads them over to the pianoforte. She wipes at their tears with her handkerchief and whispers to them in soothing tones.

"May I see my husband?" my mother asks.

"Not likely, madam." The captain looks down again at the floor.

My mother's body stiffens, but she lets go no cry. Instead she stands. "Where are we to be quartered? I need a place to put this sleeping child." Baby Rebecca has indeed fallen asleep in my mother's arms. I am glad that she, at least, is spared the anxiety of understanding our circumstance.

Captain Harkins leads us upstairs to my room, which was selected because it contains two large beds. Mother and Mary are told to bring clothing and other needed personal items from the other rooms. Captain Harkins steps out of the doorway to let them pass.

I guide Sarah and George to the window. "Watch the soldiers, and tell me what they do," I say, hoping a job will keep them from crying. Across the room is a large chest made of shiny walnut. I go there thinking to remove things from some drawers so there will be room for what Mary and Mother bring. Instead, I find myself leaning against the chest just as Captain Harkins leans against the door frame. He is looking at baby Rebecca, who sleeps on the bed. There is a soft, longing look on his face. He moves a step toward her.

For a minute I think he might touch her. I am ready to protest, but he only gazes down at her and smiles. "Boy or girl?"

"Girl." I think he is about to say more, but he doesn't.

I decide to ask some questions while Mother is not present. "Are we to be kept here, then, always prisoners in this room?"

"Oh, I think you might walk about a bit at times if you are careful to mind your mouth and stay out of the way. There are those among us who would not hesitate to run you through with a bayonet." He glances down for a moment, then goes on. "Your little sister seems a bit too bold for her own good." I feel ashamed that he does not caution me against being bold.

His seeming concern for our safety does not soften my feeling toward him, but it does encourage me to ask another question. "Will my father truly be hanged?" I ask, and my every muscle tightens as I wait for his answer.

"You think he will not join us?"

I issue a disgusted snort and shake my head with certainty.

"It is not my place, or Keegan's, to say what punishment will befall him." He sighs. "Hanging is a large possibility."

I glance quickly at Sarah and George, who are still at their post. They do not seem to have listened to our conversation.

"Joey," calls George. "Come see what the redcoats are building. What is it?"

I move to the window, but I cannot answer my little brother's question. There in our side garden, among the honeysuckle bushes, the soldiers are erecting a rough platform with a trapdoor. I am sure the wood is from my father's sawmill, and I am sure they are using that wood to build a gallows.

"I don't know what they build," I say when I am able to speak. "Likely some sort of housing. Not all those men can sleep in this house." I pull the brocaded curtains closed, take a hand of each child, and lead them away. "Why not look at storybooks?" I take two from George's shelf.

Sarah does not open her book. "I'm hungry, Joey," she says, and she rubs her tummy.

"May I go for food?" I ask, and Captain Harkins nods.

Mother and Mary are back before I leave the room. "They're building a gallows in the side garden," I whisper to Mary as I pass her, and I am ashamed that I am too frightened to keep the news to myself.

For a moment her face twists with fright, but then she tightens her lips and reaches for my hand. "Our father will not be hanged," she says. "The redcoats will not so easily defeat Joseph Kershaw."

She squeezes my hand, and courage seems to pass through her fingers to mine. I pull myself up tall again and remember that I am my father's son.

Downstairs I peer cautiously into the dining room. Soldiers, all gold-braided officers, sit around my mother's fine mahogany table. One heavy man with a dark beard leans back so that his chair balances on the back legs. I wonder that the legs have not broken. Our best pewter mugs are in the men's hands, and from the smell I know they are drinking my father's rum.

Then I catch a sight that almost makes me cry out. Two men stand just back of the table. They are throwing darts, and the target is my father's portrait, which hangs above the mantel.

Like hot water, anger rushes through me. My mouth opens to shout a protest, but I clap my hand over it. What good would my words do? I pull myself back and head toward the keeping room stairs. "You have a gun," I whisper to myself. "A day will come when you can make at least one redcoat pay."

My favorite room is different now because it is full of soldiers. Some are eating, some poke about in the supplies. Some play cards at the table where Euven and

I studied. Even the smell I love has changed. Now the odor of boot leather and sweaty bodies overpowers that of spices and tea.

Only the woodbox is unchanged. It sits, as always, beside the hearth. The pistol waits for me, still, beneath the firewood. I stand quietly, staring at the box. The time will come, I tell myself, when I throw out the logs, seize the gun, and use it. The time will come when I strike against the evil British thieves who mock my father with their darts.

Biddy is at her worktable. Like the rest of us, she is frightened. She kneads the bread with nervous jerks, and her eyes dart about the room constantly. I wish to say something that will comfort her, but the best I can offer is a weak smile.

Her fear has not made her forget us. On the table is a basket of cold meat and bread. There are also tin cups.

"Here," she whispers, and she lifts for a second the cloth that covers a crock. "I done hid this away from the morning milking. Just now brings it up from the cellar." She glances at the soldiers. "They got no business guzzling it down." She sets the crock in another basket. "You tell the mistress not to worry 'bout food. Biddy has ways."

"Thank you," I say and take a basket in each hand.

"Don't you fret either, little master. Them redbirds might perch here a bit, but they is going to fly away."

"Yes, just red birds." I will remember to tell George and Sarah to think of the soldiers as red birds. Staying close to the wall and keeping my head down, I move quickly back upstairs. Mother wakes little Rebecca, breaks the bread for her, and tears the meat into tiny pieces for the other children. "Eat, children," she urges. "We must keep our bodies strong."

I remember the soldiers rummaging through our provisions and wonder how long there will be food to keep up our strength even with Biddy's hiding. But I have other worries. Outside my window the hammering continues. Who will be hanged in our side garden?

The pounding, I realize, now seems to surround the house. I go to the window. Dozens of English soldiers labor on the grass below. They dig holes for huge poles that take three men to raise. Some men are busy nailing up support timbers.

A great stockade-type fence is going up all around us. I hate the ugly wall that shuts us off from the rest of the world. "We will tear it down," I say aloud. "When they are gone, the fence will come down." In the back of my mind I wonder how many Kershaws will be left alive when this war is over.

I turn back to the room. My mother sits with the children on the bed. George's eyes are big with fear. Even little Sarah is absolutely still except that she sucks at her thumb, a habit she gave up last year. Only the baby, who plays with the empty tin cups, is happy.

It is soon evident why the British are building a stockade. Mary and I are at the front window when we see the first of them, coming across the green and up the hill toward our house. They are staggering, bleeding American prisoners. It seems they will surely fall, but somehow the unsteady line moves forward, prodded by muskets, bayonets, and curses from the mouths of redcoats.

"Oh," says Mary. "Oh, no."

Mother, followed by George and Sarah, are beside us then. She presses her fist to her mouth as if to hold back a scream. We watch silently. Each of us, I know, is thinking of Father.

Our eyes strain for a good look at every soldier. They are all broken, even the ones without the crude bandages on their heads or limbs. Their faces tell the story of a battle lost and of watching friends die.

They keep coming and coming. I feel as if all the men of fighting age in the Carolinas are being herded into a prison made from our yard.

It is George who spots the figure first, and he points.

The soldier is near the top of the hill. He is tall. Like Father his hair is mostly gray. His movements too seem familiar. Only the stooped shoulders do not fit. But then, do they not all look beaten?

Mary grips tightly to my arm. Mother's lips move, and I know that she is praying. I am the first to realize, and I call out, "He is not Father."

"Oh," Mother whispers. "Oh, dear God, help us."

I am uncertain as to whether she is relieved or disappointed that the man walking toward us is not the master of this house. I am even unsure how I feel, but I know I should do something to ease my mother's strain. "Sit down," I say to her. "It is too hard to watch."

"They are so sad." Her eyes are dry, but there is great anguish in her voice. "We are all so sad." She leads George and Sarah back to the bed. "Call me," she says. "Call me if . . ."

"I will," I promise. I do not move from my post. Mary stands with me. Finally, just when the sun is almost down, the last downtrodden soldier is driven into our garden.

Still we watch. A large barrel is rolled into view by two redcoats. Another brings four large dippers. The barrel is opened, and the men line up for drinks. The first soldier is bent and wrinkled with age. I wonder why a man so old has gone to fight. He grabs the cup and swallows the drink in one gulp. When he moves to dip again, a redcoat snatches away the dipper and shoves the old man down onto the grass. A younger prisoner behind him bends to help the older one up.

Then he turns back for his drink, but the same redcoat pushes him on without a drop of water. The American looks at the Englishman, and for a moment I think he will strike back. Then another Englishman steps around the first and hands a cup of water to the American, who drinks it and moves on.

"Maybe they're not all bad," Mary says softly.

I shake my head. "Don't count on it. Don't you ever trust any of them, not one of the king's henchmen."

When twilight finally comes, someone in the yard below us begins to play a fiddle. We do not know where the instrument comes from. Neither Mary nor I saw a soldier carry one, but from the music we know the fiddler is an American.

"They are brave, children," my mother says. "The soldiers are beaten, but they are brave. Listen to the music."

We are quiet. When the tune changes, Mother smiles. "It's a song my mother used to sing." She goes to the window, leans on the sill, and begins to sing. "O Johnny dear has gone away, He has gone afar across the bay, O my heart is sad and weary today, Johnny has gone for a soldier. Shule, shule, shule agah, Time can only heal my woe, Since the lad of my heart from me did go, O Johnny has gone for a soldier."

Her voice is strong but gentle at the same time. Her

fair hair is let down, and the rays of the moon light her outline against the window. I think that to the suffering men below she must appear as an angel. At the chorus, she sings a line in Gaelic, the language she spoke as a small child before her family came to America.

When the song is over, the men clap and shout their thanks. Mother does not sing again, but she seems less nervous now. "We must be soldiers now too," she tells us.

With very few breaks, the haunting fiddle music continues long into the night. The fog of sleep wraps around me, but I am still aware of the music and of the soldiers that fill our back garden. Neither do I forget the gallows that stand waiting in the moonlight among the honeysuckle.

Chapter Six

Dear Father,

Are you really in Camden Jail? We can see that building from our upstairs balcony. How can you be so nearby and seem so far away?

I wake to the thud of board striking board. I turn my head toward the window, but someone has pulled the curtains. "Don't open them," says my mother from across the room, where she sits writing at the desk.

I sit up, and I realize what causes the thud. The trapdoor of the gallows strikes the back of the structure when the latch is sprung. The hanging has begun. The other children are still sleeping. Mother does not speak.

She keeps her head down, her mouth pulled straight and tight. The quill pen is gripped tightly in her hand.

Two, three, four, five, I count. There is little space between the thuds. The soldiers, I know, must be lined up on the great structure, waiting their turn to die.

How did the English decide who would die? Did they, I wondered, have some sort of trial, or were the death sentences handed out offhandedly to reduce the great number of prisoners the British had to care for?

My stomach begins to turn and then to rise. Jumping up, I run to the chamber pot. On my knees I am wretched and vomiting.

After I have washed at the bowl and pitcher, I go to my mother, who has put away her quill and folded her piece of stationery. She looks up at me and forces a smile. "We must endure, Joey," she says. "We will fall sick to our stomachs many times, even sick to our souls, but we must endure."

Later I learn that what my mother has written is a letter to my father. I wonder what she has said. Has she begged him to fight for the British, to at least pretend allegiance to the crown?

"I am going to see Cornwallis," Mother announces. She goes behind the dressing screen and changes into a bright green frock. Then she brushes her fair hair and piles it on the top of her head.

"What will you say to him?" Mary asks as she watches Mother put on a green hat.

Mother draws in a deep breath. "I shall say, General Cornwallis, you have come into my home and banished my family to one small room. Your men eat my food and leave marks upon my floor. I am here to ask, politely, to beg if you wish it. I beg that you allow me to visit my husband in Camden Jail."

It is a lovely speech, but Mother is never allowed to give it to General Cornwallis. She is told he will see her, but we wait for two hours outside the door to what was once our dining room. Soldiers come and go.

Once the general himself comes out to leave the house, but he is surrounded by other officers. "Lord Cornwallis," my mother calls out, but he does not even turn his powdered wig to glance in our direction.

My mother wants to remain until Cornwallis's return, but we are ordered back to our quarters. Finally, when he brings our noon meal of bread and cheese, Captain Harkins also brings us word. "The general says there is no time to give you an audience. Nor will he allow you to go into the jail, which is no fit place for a lady."

Mother pulls in her breath as if someone has struck her, but the captain goes on. "He will, however, allow the boy to go." He leans his head in my direction.

"Alone?" I blurt out the question before I think, and immediately my face burns with shame.

"I will go with you." Mary jumps from her seat on my bed and comes to stand beside me near the door.

"The general will not allow a grown woman to go," I say more gruffly than I should. "He would never allow a little girl to accompany me."

Mary turns to Mother. "Let me dress like a boy in some of Joey's clothes. I am almost as tall as he is."

Mother does not even consider the request, and I am ashamed that I wish she would. Mary is plucky. Having her beside me would give me heart.

I am too unsettled even to taste the cheese or bread. While the others eat, I move about the room, trying not to pace the same spot.

Mother has folded the letter to Father, and she presses it into my hand when it is time for me to go. "Wait until he has read it if they will allow you to tarry so long," she says. "He may want to give a word or two as reply."

Our porch is now full of redcoats. They see me as I make my way out the door, but they do not step aside to let me pass. I pull myself up straight. "Excuse me, here," I say, but my words come out much fainter than I intended. A soldier elbows me, and I fall sideways into another redcoat.

"There, now, little Yankee boy, watch your step."

He shoves me into yet another man, who is dark, with mean eyes.

"I say," the thin soldier shouts, "what have we here? A bit of a ball to play with?" He shoves me back in the direction from which I came.

A third man grabs me now. There is a vile smell of strong drink on his breath, which he blows into my face as he speaks. "A letter, have you? Let's have a look-see."

He reaches for the papers. I scream, and with a mighty swing I kick at him.

My foot finds its mark, and there is now a streak of dirt on the white leg of his uniform. "You little rebel devil," he shouts, and he spreads the palm of his big hand, ready to slap my face.

I am unaware that Captain Harkins has stepped out onto the porch until he bellows, "Desist." The man who holds me loosens his grip at once. I stumble and almost fall among the men, who are suddenly quiet. "Attention," shouts the captain, and they stand straight and salute.

The captain takes my arm and pulls me away from the others, at whom he glares. "Your behavior is disgraceful. Does the king's army have nothing more to do than torment children? You are now warned. Should I see or hear again of any such behavior, I will see that the offender or offenders . . ." He pauses and looks about at each face. "I personally will see that you are thrown into Camden Jail and left to the mercy of the rebel soldiers there."

The men are quiet. Without looking up, I say, "Thank you, Captain Harkins," and I hurry down the steps. Another redcoat passes me on the first step. I do not look up at his face, but when he speaks to the captain, I recognize his voice. "You won't always be about to rescue them," says Keegan. I turn back and see his beastly grin.

On the bottom step, I stop and stare. A mound of newly dug earth is spread across the grass where a big ditch has been dug in front of our house. It is covered over now, but I know it serves as a grave for the men hanged this morning.

Don't think, I tell myself. Don't think at all. Just walk by the ditch with your eyes on the poplar tree. There is a robin in the poplar tree, and she sings as she builds her nest.

So fastened on the bird and her song am I that at first I do not hear Captain Harkins calling, "Young Joseph." I stop, but I do not turn back, which would mean seeing the ditch again. He comes to stand beside me. "You have an order of passage from General Cornwallis." He points to the paper I hold with Mother's letter. "Use it." He looks back toward the men on the porch. "Soldiers will soon enough part when they see the seal."

For just a moment gratitude makes me feel warm toward the captain, but then I remember the uniform he wears. The warm feelings turn to ice. "Thank you," I say, and I walk away from him.

"Wait," he calls. "I may as well go with you a ways, give my legs a bit of stretch."

I think I should not be happy of any Brit's company, but I am. I do not say so, however, and we walk in silence.

The Camden I knew is gone, turned into a different town. I am amazed at how quickly the British soldiers have made it their own. Though the day is fair as only a June day may be, no children chase hoops through the streets. Women in gingham dresses do not pause before the shops with their baskets to exchange a bit of gossip with one another. Men do not stand about the doorways of the blacksmith shop or the tavern. Instead there are redcoats everywhere. Those citizens who do stir move quickly, eyes down. Even the dogs seem unnerved, slinking near their homes, tails between their legs.

Euven is standing in front of the Quaker meeting hall. I run to him. "They hang men." My words are soft, but inside I am screaming. "They dig big ditches in our front yard. Just toss in the bodies and cover them up."

For a moment Euven closes his eyes. He presses his

fingertips against the sides of his face. Finally, he speaks. "War is never kind, Joey," he says, and he reaches out to touch my shoulder before he leans against the wall of the church.

"They're murderers." I clench both my fists. "I wish I could hang every one of them."

Then Captain Harkins is beside me. "You've found a friend then, young Joseph?"

"Yes," I mutter without looking at him."Euven is my teacher."

Euven steps forward and introduces himself. Captain Harkins says his name, and Euven puts out his hand, as if the captain has come to our village on holiday, a pleasant visitor.

I am horrified to see an American so welcoming. "Euven is a Quaker," I explain. "He does not believe in war."

"Perhaps we should all become Quakers," Captain Harkins says, and his smile seems sad.

"I wish to seek permission to come to Kershaw House to go on with Joey's lessons. I've been paid in advance."

I am disgusted with Euven for being so friendly to the enemy. I keep my eyes down so that he will not see how much I want to go on with lessons. Having him come to the house each day would be a comfort and a distraction, and I am hopeful.

Captain Harkins is all soldier again. "It is Cornwallis House now," he says. "I will need to check orders, but come tomorrow. It is probable the way will have been cleared by then."

Euven nods, then smiles at me and gives my shoulder a friendly slap. Captain Harkins and I move on, but I look back at Euven. I am very glad he will be each day in our house. As I watch, Hannah Goodnight comes from the meetinghouse door. Her golden hair shines in the sun. Euven steps toward her, and they stand smiling into each other's eyes. For a moment the thought that war does not change everything warms me.

But the warmth cannot last. The jail looms before me. I am afraid, afraid of seeing my father as a prisoner, afraid to face him because I failed to save my mother and the little ones from the British.

At the low wooden steps Captain Harkins stops and tells me to show my pass to the guards at the entrance. "I will wait here for you," he says, and he takes a pipe from his haversack.

My knees are shaking, but I step up to the big door and to the guards. They look only at the seal. "Tell them inside what business you have," the taller one says.

I pull open the heavy door, and I am horrified. This small jail was never meant to be a military prison. It is full of men, most of them in shackles. They sit upon the floor everywhere. A few are stretched out, eyes closed. I wonder if they are asleep or dead.

The talking and the moaning mix and become one mournful lament. There is a smell of sickness and of human waste. The guards who surround the men look as miserable as do their prisoners.

"How did you get in here?" a guard demands. He points at my chest with the sharpest, shiniest bayonet I've ever seen. My skin stings as I imagine how that blade could slice.

"A pass from General Cornwallis," I say. I hold it out, and I try to keep my hand steady. "I've come to see my father." I do not step back, but I am glad when he finally lowers his bayonet.

"And who might that be?"

"Joseph Kershaw."

He points toward a corner staircase. "Up there."

I make my way through the broken men. Most of them ignore me, but one reaches out to touch my leg. He is older than most of the others, probably as old as my father. His face is flushed, and I believe he is ill. "Please lad," he mumbles, "could you get me word of my . . ."

I can hear no more. His voice is too weak to compete with the sounds all about us. I hunch down closer to his face, but a guard is coming toward us. "You, boy," he shouts. "No talking to the prisoners. Get on to your business."

The soldier does not turn loose of my leg at once, but I pull away and move on. I turn to look back. He is bent, head on his knees, and the guard is coming toward him with a wooden club in his hand. Quickly, I look away, facing the stairs again. If the guard strikes the man, I cannot bear to see.

Moving toward the stairs, I keep my gaze down, determined not to look into the eyes of another prisoner. My own misery is enough. I have no strength for viewing another's.

Twelve big steps make up the stairs to the second floor. Counting them helps calm my pounding heart. Unlike the crowded lower floor, there are cells here, but many men are crowded into each one. I stretch my neck trying to search out my father. A guard comes to me at once. I do not see his face at all because I study the buttons on his uniform. Yet somehow I am aware of his scowl, and that his expression is full of disgust. I hold out the piece of paper, at which he only glances.

"Miserable yokels," he mutters, "why do they let them in here?" He does not seem to be talking to me, but he knows I can hear his insult.

My hand tightens into a fist, but I know that I have just used that hand to hold my entry permission. I push back my thoughts about how this jail belonged to the people of Camden long before redcoats such as this ill-tempered soldier came along. I do not wish to make him dislike me so much that he might throw me out despite my pass.

The guard begins to move, and I follow him through a hallway that leads to another group of cells. Without a word he points toward a middle cage made of iron bars.

There is my father. His head is down, and he does not see me. But his face is in full view. I gasp and am unconcerned by the snort of disapproval made by the guard. Father has turned old, older perhaps than the soldier who tried to talk to me. Is it possible that his hair has always had so much gray? Could his face have been so lined before? I shake my head. No, this defeat has aged Joseph Kershaw the elder!

I do not want to walk up to him. He sits in chains with his head bowed. My father has never bowed his head to anyone but God. I will not tell my mother how he looks. I will lie and say he seems strong.

The guard prods me with the butt of his musket. "Want to see him or not?" he says before he stomps off.

I step closer. "Father," I say, but I know my voice is too soft. "Father," I say again, and this time he hears me. He gets up from the bench and comes toward the front bars. Watching him hobble with the chains is almost too much for me.

"Young Joseph," he calls. "My son is here." The other prisoners sit up and take notice, but soon I am aware only of my father. His face has lost most of the weariness now. It is you who makes the difference, I tell myself. You are your father's son, and you bring hope to him.

His chained hands grip the bars, and I reach out to touch one of them briefly. I would like to lay my face against his fingers to feel his touch, but I do not. Such an act would be acceptable for Mary or George, but not for me, for I am now a man.

"You are safe," he says. "Your mother, the other children?"

"We are all well." I swallow. "The redcoats have taken over our house, put us in a room upstairs. The town did not even try to fight them."

He nods. "There was no way. If a small regiment had come . . ." He stops and shakes his head slowly. "But the devils are everywhere, behind every tree, sitting on every step." His voice drops. "There was never any hope of defeating them."

Defeat is not a word I have ever associated with my father, but as if he reads my mind, he pulls his body straighter. "The war is not over yet, son," he says. For a second I feel better, glad to see him unconquered, but then he adds, "We'll win. We'll get rid of those red-coats, and you can help."

"I can help?" I stare at him with disbelief. Had he not just commented on the vastness of their number?

"You watch." He grips the bars hard, and his eyes drill into me. "You watch for a chance to strike against the murdering, thieving lobster backs. Be vigilant, and your chance will come."

I nod my head, and I say, "I will, Father. I promise I will watch."

He smiles. I feel good. There beside my father I am confident that I will not fail his charge.

Then my father's expression changes. "Son," he says gently. "I think they have let you come today because it is my last day in this prison."

"No," the scream comes out without my willing it to, and I wipe my hand across my eyes, trying to erase the picture of the gallows that flashes before them.

"Easy, boy. I'm to be put on a ship, sent to an island prison, Bermuda perhaps."

My knees are weak with relief. "I thought . . . Father, they've built a gallows in our side garden and this morning they hanged men, many of them."

"In my garden! They hang Carolina's defenders on my very property!"

"Among the honeysuckle," I add as if the detail were an important one.

My father's face now has no trace of old age or defeat. It is red, burning with hate. "By God, we shall show them!"

"Are you sure they won't kill you?"

He is still angry and shakes his head vigorously. "They know I've still some important friends in England. They'll save me for trading. When the war is over, they'll want me to exchange for officers and such."

Suddenly I remember. "Mother sent this," I say, and I yank the letter from my pocket to hold out to him.

"Your mother," he says, and he looks surprised, as if maybe she had slipped his mind. "Oh, give me the letter." He is still reading when I hear the drums. A small group of six or so men come marching into the room.

"They're here," my father says and he begins to speak very rapidly. "Cornwallis wanted me to join the damnable British, actually thought I might." He squeezes my hands. "See to your mother and the others. Tell them not to worry. I shall likely be allowed to write to you all."

I hate the tear that forces its way from my eye, and down my cheek. My father, I hope, has not noticed. He straightens his worn uniform and tightens back the binding, which has let his hair fall loose about his face. He does this, I know, for the soldiers who served beneath him. He has no wish to appear as a beggar when the British march him out.

"Be brave, my son, and be vigilant for your chance to strike," he says, and he smiles at me.

They are beside me now. "Step aside," bellows an officer, and I catch the flash of his bayonet in the sunlight from a high window. A young soldier produces a key. The door is opened, and my father and his cellmates are yanked out.

"Wait," I scream and try to slip around a large soldier to reach my father. The soldier does not look at me, but his red-sleeved elbow jams hard into my ribs.

I fall back against the cell bars, but I get a glimpse of my father's face. "Stand tall, young Joseph Kershaw," he calls. Then they are marching him away. My father looks back, but an extended bayonet forces him to turn again.

All around the jail our soldiers are shouting messages. "Cheers for Colonel Kershaw!"

"God be with you, Sir!"

"Carolina salutes you!"

Still leaning against the bars, I slide down and let myself settle in a miserable heap upon the floor. My father is out of sight now, and no pass will allow me to see him. They are taking him across the ocean, and I wonder if ever he will return.

From a corner of the jail one lone voice starts to

sing. "Come join hand in hand, brave Americans all, And rouse your bold hearts at fair Liberty's call, No tyrannous acts shall suppress your just claim, Or stain with dishonour America's name."

Other singers join. Looking about, I see several soldiers who, like me, have raised their bent heads. Many of them are singing now. Most of these men are bound hand and foot. They are in danger of being hanged. Yet they sing.

I have the strength now to rise and am about to do so when I stop, suddenly aware that a red leg is beside me. Looking up, I see the young soldier. He goes into the cell once occupied by my father. It occurs to me now to wonder what will become of the two men who were crowded in with my father. Will they too be shipped off to prison, or are they even now waiting in our side yard to be hanged?

The young soldier has picked up my father's knapsack. I know that the bag contains things my father will need, one of them being a box with a lock of my mother's hair tied with a blue ribbon.

"Will you take the bag to him?" I ask.

The soldier nods his head, and I see that his expression is kind. "That I will," he says. "Me own father is in an American prison. Would that some soldier there be kind to him."

He dashes away, leaving me staring after him. For a

moment I think about Euven's remark that not all red-coats are monsters, but I do not let the thought fully form. There is far too much for me to do. I cannot let myself be distracted by thinking of kind redcoats.

I am up then and making my way to the door. Men wave to me with shackled hands and call encouraging words. Near the door sits a boy who is certainly about my own age. His hair is red, and his face is freckled. On his cheek is a great bloody slash.

He glances up at me, and I lean down to him. "Are you a soldier?" I ask.

"Reckon I am now." His voice is full of fire.

Beside him is a youth who is somewhat older, but who bears so strong a resemblance to the first that I am sure they are brothers. It is the older one who speaks next. "He was but walking beside me along the road after the battle. The lousy lobster backs slapped him in chains and threw him in here with the lot of us, him just an innocent boy."

"Old enough to face a redcoat's saber," the boy says, and I see that he is proud of the injury.

His brother is proud too. "Refused to black the nasty colonel's British boots." He smiles, but then turns serious. "Wound needs dressing, though." He uses his head to point to a shelf beside the door. "There's ban-dages and cleaning solution right there, but not one guard will lift a finger to help."

A snort comes from the injured boy. "I'd not have a redcoat bandaging any spot on me. Likely their very hands are poison."

"I'll do it." I start to move away, but the boy grabs at my trousers. "Do they come and sight you they're liable to do as bad to you as they did to me."

I look directly into his steady eyes. "Let them do it, then," I say. "We're all likely to bear the hateful mark of the British in one way or another."

It seems certain that the guards see me take the materials from the shelf and carry it back to begin the dressing, but no one moves to stop me. "They're about half asleep," I comment on the guards as I work.

The boy's left hand, cut to the bone, is even worse than the injury on the cheek, which is what I first noticed. "I put it up to ward off the blow," he says as I clean the gash.

I am not experienced as a nurse. The raw, gaping flesh makes my stomach roll, but I do not give up until a rough bandage covers both spots.

The brothers tell me they are from over Waxhaw way and that their surname is Jackson. They talk too about why they fight. "We're a new country," says the older one. "Don't want to bow down to kings on account of who his father was."

"Don't want to bow down to any man." The younger one makes a fist with his uninjured hand.

"Guess you've proved that," I say.

The older one nods his head. "You mark the name Andy Jackson. There's a flame in my brother, there is, and I'll tell you the world is bound to see it."

Andy laughs. "The British will see it for sure. If ever I get out of here, I'll fell me more than one of His Majesty's henchmen."

Both brothers thank me. I return the supplies to the shelf, but I am drawn back to the Jacksons. "Perhaps I'll see you again," I say.

"God willing, we may be side by side and fighting the British one day," says the injured one.

I go down the stairs with a burning inside me, a flame built upon the promise to my father and lit from the fire of Andrew Jackson. I will watch, as my father has told me, for every chance to strike against the cruel enemy. Perhaps I, like Andy Jackson, will bring down a redcoat.

Moving again through the huddled prisoners, I feel much stronger. I meet their eyes, and I wave my hand or nod my head. Some of them smile at me, and I feel they know somehow that I too am at war with the British.

When I see the soldier who wanted to speak to me, I know that I will try again. I make my way through the others toward him. A guard, from his corner post, shouts at me, but I flash the seal. "Permission from Lord Cornwallis," I call. He yawns and makes no effort to move toward me.

The soldier sits hunched, knees raised to support his head and arms. He does not see me. I touch the torn sleeve of his dirty shirt. "Hello," I say softly, but he does not lift his head.

I glance at the spot where the guard stands, but he seems to pay me no mind. Still, another, more diligent than this tired, round man, may come at any moment. There is not a moment to waste. This time I put my hand on his shoulder. Through the rough material of his shirt, I can feel heat, too much even to be caused by being crowded in this hot jail.

"Fever," I say and I give him a gentle shake. There is a small moan as he raises his head and looks at me with weak, watery eyes.

"I'm terrible sick, boy."

"Someone should help you." I glance around at the other men, also in shackles.

He raises his hand to give a feeble motion of dismissal. "It's my boy I'm fretted over. We was in the battle together, but I ain't seen him since. Rob's his name. Rob Wilson. I've passed the word all about. He ain't here. What's become of him? That's what I've got to know."

I stare at the frail soldier whose life is likely slipping away, but whose only concern is for his son. "I'll find out for you," I promise.

"You're a good lad," he whispers, and he drops his head back to his arms.

Just as I feared, another guard has joined the round one and has been informed of my pass. "Boy," shouts the new one. "Get over here. I'll have me a look-see at Lord Cornwallis's seal."

I begin to wind around the soldiers, and I am aware that both guards watch me with eyes full of scorn. When I reach them, I say nothing, only hold out the paper.

The round one takes it, and they both study the paper. Something about the way they examine the seal makes me believe that neither of them can read. I force myself to make no insulting remark about their ignorance. Instead I say, "May I go now?"

"Reckon you can run along now, sonny," says the round one. He returns my paper, and then with an ugly laugh he adds, "Hope you reach your journey's end before the pox overtakes you."

"What?" I look at him with wonder. "Why do you say such a thing?"

The other slaps at his knee with mirth. "That rebel, him what you was talking to. Reckon he has the pox. Lots of them does."

"Yeah, that's right, sonny." The round one points to his own scarred face. "That's why the likes of me and Johnson here gets the job of guarding the poor beggers. We done had the pox."

The horror I feel must be evident on my face because their laughter grows stronger. It follows me across the crowded floor and out the door.

Captain Harkins leans against the porch rail as he waits. I am ashamed because the sight of him makes me feel better. Inwardly scolding myself for finding comfort in the presence of the enemy, I scowl when he smiles at me.

"How is your father?" he asks, and we begin to walk down the sandy street.

"My father is well." I straighten my shoulders and head, pulling myself up tall and trying to quiet my pounding heart. "My father is strong, and he is not defeated." I do not glance at the captain, who is my enemy, and we move through what was once the familiar village of Camden in silence.

When we are near Kershaw House, I see the lines of soldiers in the side yard again, and I see the gallows. The hangings are about to begin once more. I stop as if suddenly frozen. I will not hide my face this time.

The captain takes my arms and leads me toward the front steps. "Upstairs with you now," he says, and he opens the door. Inside, I press against the wall, listening. The thuds, familiar from the morning, begin. Men are dying.

I draw in a breath and step back through the door. There are no redcoats on the porch. I go to the railing and, leaning over, I can see into the side garden. Four guards are there, muskets and bayonets pointing at the soldiers who, eyes down, wait.

Last in line is a young man. He is tall and his thin face is partially covered by the straggly beginnings of a beard. They should have let him shave before his execution, I think.

The guard who is at the last of the line is one whose face I recognize from the earlier encounter, one who Captain Harkins ordered to leave me be.

I know what must be done. With my hands clenched into a fist, I move toward the gallows.

"Halt!" the redcoat shouts.

Halt I do, but I fold my arms and speak gruffly. "Leave me alone," I say in what I hope is a determined voice. "I have Captain Harkins's permission to be here and Lord Cornwallis's own seal." I flash the paper in his direction.

The soldier hesitates. I consider reminding him of the captain's threat, but I think better of it. "I only want to speak to the men," I say.

The guard shrugs his shoulders, and I go quickly to

the young soldier. "Rob Wilson," I say. "Do you know him?"

With manacled hands, he pointed in front of him. "Third one up," he says in a voice that sounds already dead. "You'd better hurry."

Before I can move, though, he speaks again. This time there is life in his voice. "Are you a friend?" he asks. I nod. "My mother," he says in a rush, "Sarah Jenkins is her name, lives over by Sander's Creek. I'm James. Will you get word to her, please?" His voice almost breaks, but he swallows and goes on. "She'll hate it powerful bad, but still she ought to know. Don't you reckon?"

With a start, I realize he is waiting for an answer from me. "Yes, she ought to know."

"You'll see to it, then?"

"Yes. Sarah Jenkins by Sander's Creek."

"Bless you. God bless you." Before I turn, I see a smile come to his lips.

Running, I call, "Rob Wilson?"

"Yes," says the third man from Jenkins, and he pauses to turn toward me.

Suddenly the guard is beside him, bayonet thrust forward. "Move on," he shouts.

The prisoner walks, and I trot to get beside him. "I've word from your father," I tell him. "He worries for you."

"My father," he repeats. The two words come slowly as if he tastes them well before letting go. He turns his head so that I get one glimpse of his face. His eyes are blue, like those of his father, but clear and untroubled by sickness. "Tell him I died well. Tell him I did not beg."

"Yes," I say, and I stop walking, as he moves forward.

He turns back for another glance. "Is he wounded?"

"No." Without deciding to do so, I lie. "Your father is well."

"Good," he says, and now he is at the steps of the gallows.

I want to turn away. I have managed to block out the sight of the other men and the sounds of their deaths, and I do not want to watch Rob Wilson die.

My feet start to move, but I force them to stay. As he climbs the steps, I suck in my breath and hold it. Just before he reaches the top step, I am forced to breathe again. I whisper a little prayer, but I do not bow my head or close my eyes. I will watch Rob Wilson die, and I will not be sick to my stomach. I am different from the boy who vomited this morning.

Now I too am a soldier. I will not cry. I will not be sick. I will wait, and I will watch. The chance will come for me to strike back for Rob Wilson and the other men who die among the blooms in my side yard.

Even when it is over for Rob, I stay until James Jenkins too has stepped to his death. Now there is something I can tell my own father. I can tell him that these sons of Carolina did not die alone.

I do not stay to watch the men carried to the long ditch in front of the house. Inside me there is a great sadness and a great anger. I whirl away from the gallows and tromp back toward the front of the house. One of the guards steps out toward me as if to speak. I glare into his eyes, but I do not slow my pace. He says nothing, and I stomp around him.

The porch is no longer empty. Three redcoats lounge on the steps playing cards. Unaffected by the burials, they laugh and talk together. "I've got me eye on one or two of them pretty Camden maidens," a fat soldier says.

"The major ordered us to leave them be." His small companion stretches and yawns.

"Leave them be, huh! You just watch how I leave them be."

All three of them laugh. There is space enough between the two smaller men for me to get up the steps. I duck my head and charge in that direction.

"Wait, little fellow. You didn't say the password," the big one says, and he laughs. The smaller one grabs my leg. I kick at him and stumble on through the front door.

The big one is behind me. I throw myself at the stairs, but the soldier's hand reaches out and grabs me.

"Leave my brother alone!" It is Mary's voice. I know that she stands about halfway up the stairs, but I do not look at her. I turn to face the redcoat.

"You rebel brat." He reaches out and grabs my collar. I spit at him, and his heavy hand flies to slap me, leaving the left side of my cheek burning.

"Watkins!" Captain Harkins shouts. He too is on the stairs. The soldier lets go of me, and I run. Up the steps I go, and without slowing down I try to pass Captain Harkins. "Joey," he says. I want to ignore him and push around him, but there is no railing. Reaching out, he locks his hand over my shoulder. "I'm sorry. Those men will go on report."

I do not struggle with him. Instead I turn to meet his gaze. "Joey is a nickname used by friends," I say coldly. "Please call me Joseph."

Chapter Seven

Dear Father,

*I am changed. Yes, I am still afraid, but I am more angry.
I have stood beside the gallows and watched our men die.*

*The slaves are all gone except Cato and Biddy. Cato
says they are probably hiding in the woods. When I said to
Biddy that I appreciate how she did the right thing and
did not run away, she laughed. Then she said, "Master
Joey, yo' sure don't understand very much, not very much
a' tall."*

It is now my habit to rise early. Leaving Mother
and the others still sleeping, I slip from our room
and head for the upstairs veranda. From there I can see
the town. I look each day for some change, something
that might give me hope. I notice too the natural things

that have always been part of my world but that are more dear to me now that I am a prisoner.

The July sun is already hot. The early morning fog has been burned away except along the Wateree River. There is a cornfield, tall and green. "Carolina corn," I say, "growing near the river." I find strength in the corn and the river with its fog.

I do not keep my eyes turned toward the river. Instead I look back toward the town. What I see makes me shiver despite the sun. Five men are being carried up the hill on litters. I know even before I recognize the big scarred guard that the soldiers are victims of smallpox.

The horrible disease is coming toward us. As if I could protect my family, I run back inside. My mother is up now, and she too is watching the procession. I go to stand beside her at the window.

"The little quarters in the back," I whisper. "That must be where they're headed."

"But why? They have not carried other injured men here." Mother turns then and studies my face. "You know, don't you, Joey?"

There is no use trying to hide the truth. "Smallpox," I say.

My mother gasps, but then we are quiet, watching. When she speaks she is calm. "The poor creatures." She slips her arm through mine. "You must not go near them. Not under any circumstances."

I nod my agreement, but I have spotted the old soldier who wanted so much to know about his son. His arm hangs over the side of the litter as he is passed under my window. He's still alive, I think, and still wondering about his boy. I will find it difficult to keep my word to my mother.

Later in the day, I do receive one bit of good news. Euven is indeed coming for lessons. I go to the keeping room, and while I wait for him at the round table I write a letter. The great doors are closed with a British guard posted in front of them outside. Euven will pass through the front door and come down the stairs.

I keep my eyes in that direction and leap to my feet when I see his boots. Then his head comes into sight. It is bent because the doorway at the bottom of the stairs is not high.

"Euven," I say, "will you help me?" I grab the letter I have written and hold it out to him.

"What's this?"

"A letter. It's to Mistress Jenkins out by Sander's Creek about her son, James."

Euven's face grows somber as he reads my words about how James thought of his mother just before he died and asked me to see that she knew of his fate. I wrote too of how he stood tall on the gallows and of how I stayed to watch until it was over.

"You expressed yourself well," he says, "and your hand has improved." He gives the letter back to me.

I scowl, impatient, that Euven wishes to discuss penmanship, evaluating my letter as a teacher when I have asked for his help. Perhaps he does not understand. "But how can I have the message delivered?"

"Why not ask Captain Harkins?"

Obviously Euven has taken leave of his senses. "Harkins? You suppose a redcoat will aid me?"

He shrugs and takes his seat, ready for the lesson. "Only a redcoat can pass through the lines. Besides, they are not all monsters."

I pound my fist against the table. "Have you not seen the gallows? Do you not know any of the men who have been hanged in my mother's side garden?"

"One, Matthew Murphy, was my boyhood friend who turned from our Quaker ways."

I see grief in his eyes and think I am about to make my point. "Have we not read, 'It is the dead who make the longest demands'?"

Slowly he nods his head. "Thee are right. Matthew's death demands me to stand for peace."

I am too furious to speak and without looking at Euven, I drop to my chair, where I slump and lean against the table.

"There are other soldiers out there who need letters written. Perhaps the captain could arrange for thee to write them." He smiles. "Doubtless he would be more quick to agree were thee also to serve those British soldiers who cannot read or write."

I let out an angry snort. "Never. I'll never be a friend to a redcoat."

Euven opens the geometry book and begins our lesson. A small smile moves across his lips, and I think that he is amused to have used the hated geometry to end our discussion.

When lessons are over and Euven has gone, I do not leave the keeping room. Instead I linger at the table, studying the woodbox. The British cook accepts my filling of it each day, probably thinking I have been assigned the task. I long to move the logs, to hold the gun in my hands for just a moment.

No one is in the keeping room except me. I rise and walk to the box. Surely it would not hurt just to touch the pistol, to reassure myself that it is real and that one day I will use my father's pistol to strike back.

But someone is coming down the stairs. It is Captain Harkins who appears. He looks at me and smiles his greeting as if I had never made the comment about the use of my name.

I feel anger growing inside me. Does he think me only a child whose rage can be forgotten the next day? I force down such thoughts. There is no way to have this letter delivered except through Captain Harkins.

I take the letter from the table and hold it out to him. "I wrote this for a soldier who was hanged yesterday. Is there hope that it could be delivered?"

"You are asking a favor of me, a man whom you despise?" He does not sound hateful.

I tell myself that if I am nice to him, I may get my way, but I can only come out with, "I ask for the dead soldier and his mother who is all alone."

He smiles. "I have a mother. It shall be delivered." Captain Hawkins moves past me toward the big doors at the front.

"There is more." He glances back and I blurt out my request. "I seek permission to write letters for other soldiers and to have them delivered or posted."

He raises his eyebrows and begins to tap the front of his boot against the brick floor. "That is a request I cannot promise will be granted."

I swallow hard. "I am willing to write for your men as well."

"Well," he says, "in such a case, we might just be able to reach an agreement. I will speak of the request to my superior."

"Thank you." I turn toward the stairs then and dash up them as quickly as possible.

And so I become a scribe. Captain Harkins has arranged it for me. The first letter was for the dying David Wilson. Mindful of my mother's request, I sat just outside the open door, where I strained to catch his words and wrote the message to his wife and daughters at home.

"My sons all be soldiers," he told me. "Oldest four marched off after we come in from the field one day to find thieving redcoats had took our cow and calf, pigs too, and bags of grain. Rob, he was the youngest." His weak voice broke into a sob, but he collected himself and went on. "We begged him out of going with his brothers, but we couldn't hold him long, him determined like he was to run the British out of Carolina. When his time come, I up and went by his side." He rested for a moment, then went on. "I pray the others yet live. You watch for the Wilson boys, will you, lad? You watch for my sons."

When I came next to the outbuilding, David Wilson was no more. The others died quickly too, as I am sure the British planned they should. Now the building stands empty, a reminder of the horrors of smallpox. Even though I never entered the quarters I scrubbed myself in an outside tub after each time of going close. There would be, for me, no desire to live if somehow I carried smallpox upstairs to my mother or to the little ones who throw their arms about my legs and squeal greetings when I enter.

Mary has joined my letter-writing efforts. I thought it too dangerous for a girl child, but Mary pleaded. Mother surprised me by giving her consent. "This war has changed us all, Joey," she said, and she put down her needlework to draw both Mary and me to her. "You two, I know, can never be children again."

At first Mary disliked writing for the redcoats as much as I do, but of late I have seen her smile at some of the British. Today I brought my bag of completed letters into the keeping room to leave for Captain Harkins to post. Mary is reading a letter to a British soldier, who sits at the table. He is the military cook whom Biddy now assists.

I hear him groan and turning, I see that he has leaned his head on the big table. Mary is up and she pats him gently on the shoulder. "I'm sorry," she says gently. "Just so awfully sorry, Sergeant Glen."

For one frightening moment, I think she is going to embrace the redcoat. I drop my letters on the shelf. "Mary," I say sternly, "Mother wishes to see you upstairs at once."

I stomp up the stairs, but it is a few minutes before my sister follows me, and I know she has lingered with the sergeant. When I open the door to our room, I hear my mother laugh. It is a sound I had not expected to hear, and I am shocked.

Biddy and Mother sit at the tiny table in the corner.

They drink tea, and I catch a phrase or two of the story Biddy is telling about a redcoat chasing a chicken in an effort to kill it. Mother and Biddy are both enjoying the tale.

I pause just inside and get right to my business. "Mother, something must be done with Mary. I have just seen her try to comfort a redcoat." I turn to close the door, but my sister is there, panting.

"The poor man's son has been killed, fighting in New York." She reaches back to slam the door with her foot. "Mother, you did not ask me to come up here as Joey claimed, did you?" Mary moves toward Mother and almost tumbles over Sarah and George, who are on the floor building with blocks.

"You should forbid her to talk to them if she is going to become friendly with the filthy . . ." I am about to use a word Mother would not like. I swallow. "I think Mary is too young to be among the enemy."

Mother flashes a frown at me. "Hush, Joey," she says. Then she turns to Mary. "What is the problem here?"

"I read Sergeant Glen a letter from his wife, sending him word of his son's death."

"Joey, surely you cannot object to your sister showing compassion," Mother says.

"They are the enemy," I shout. "I pray they will all die."

"Oh, Joey, no." Mother's voice is more sad than angry.

"Poor man," adds Biddy. "He be often talking of that boy."

They have joined together against me. I shrug my shoulders. "Waste your sympathy if you choose, but I'll save mine for my countrymen who are hanged beneath our window."

"Redbirds, blackbirds, all birds loves their baby birds just the same," says Biddy.

I am tempted to comment that if my father were here she would not be sitting drinking tea with the mistress, but I am not foolish enough to push Mother too far.

When Biddy leaves, I decide to try Mother again. She is still at the table and I join her. She smiles at me. "Biddy has promised shepherd's pie for supper. She's got a pan baking just for us."

Shepherd's pie is a favorite of mine. Mother thinks the promise of something more than cheese for our evening meal will distract me. It does not. "I am glad Biddy eases your distress," I say.

"She knows how to laugh even now," says Mother.

"Of course, she does not suffer as we do. A slave is a slave, war or not."

Mother reaches out to put her hand over mine. "Biddy knows suffering, Joey. Your father bought her for me because she was being sold away from her husband over near Waxhaw. I saw her on the auction block and felt sorry for her, wanted to keep her near. She had a babe in her arms, a little girl just the age of my James."

"What became of the child?"

"Died one night in her sleep." Mother's eyes close for a moment. "It was summer, and I woke to Biddy's screams coming from the quarter. I went to her. Our friendship began so."

"She is lucky to have found so kind a mistress," I say.

Mother shakes her head. "No, Joey, I can't say a human being who is bought and sold is lucky. Do you know what I heard another woman slave tell Biddy about the baby?"

She does not wait for my response, but her voice grows low. " 'Well, that be one sweet brown baby won't ever have her heart ripped out when they sells her from her Mammy's arms.' Sixteen years ago that was, but I can hear those words still, every syllable and tone just as they were spoken." Mother gets up to walk about, but she has more to say. "I am pondering a return to my Quaker beliefs. When this war is over, I may see that all slaves in this house are freed."

I do not say so, but I am thinking that my father will have no part of such a foolish idea. Nor would he want any member of his family to befriend a redcoat. I look at Mary, who is now on the floor with George and Sarah. She feels my gaze and glances up.

Her expression is still angry. "Not all redcoats are cruel men, Joey. I want them to lose the war and give back our house. I want Father to come home, but they are not all bad men."

"Captain Harkins has a child, a baby boy whom he has never seen," says Mother from across the room.

My anger explodes. "He should go home then. We most certainly do not need him here." Jumping up, I accidentally knock over my chair, but I do not pick it up. I dash for the door and go out onto the veranda. "Come home, Father," I shout into the blue sky. "Come home and set them straight."

Chapter Eight

Dear Father,

Cornwallis has ridden away on his great white horse with drums and bugles sounding. He is off to fight the ragged troops that try to rid South Carolina of the mighty English army.

His replacement here, Lord Rawdon, proves to be even more cruel. Our family was rounded up, told to take only what we could carry with us. It was the horrible Keegan who came for us. When George stumbled with his basket, Keegan prodded him with a musket, and he took pleasure in our dismay at being moved into the tiny quarters where men had recently died with smallpox. Mother, of course, protested.

At once Captain Keegan was beside her. "My lady does not take to the prescribed new home?" He gave her a mocking bow. "It was suggested to Lord Rawdon that you might react just so. Shall I repeat to you how His Lordship replied?" His hideous laugh interrupted his words, and he slapped at his leg with mirth. " 'Tell Mistress Kershaw,' says he, 'that the gallows stand ready if she prefers them for her brats.' "

For a long moment, Mother said nothing. Instead she stared directly into the face of Captain Keegan. "I wonder, sir, what manner of man you are," she said at last, "and if ever a mother has loved you." Then she reached for the valise she had set down, and she marched on toward the door of that death cabin.

I am about to make one good strike back.

★ We sit on the steps of the smallpox cabin. One soldier is left outside the tiny building to guard us. At least Captain Keegan does not stay. My mother insists that we sit here while she looks about inside. We have barely settled when Cato appears with hot water, soap, and rags.

My mother comes to the door. She is surprised. "They allowed you to come?" she asks Cato.

"I did not ask their permission, mistress." His dark eyes dance with defiance.

Mother and Cato scrubbed the floors and walls of our new quarters. "I will never use those mattresses," Mother says, but she will not allow me to help with the carrying. Instead when Cato hoists one end, my mother manages the other as well as could any man.

"Reckon Mr. Lord Rawdon wanting these for his bed?" says Cato, and we all laugh.

It is now night. We are settled upon the floor. "Not possible to put hands on the household bedclothes," Cato apologized, but he produced blankets for us, which he managed somehow to secure from the very supplies of the British.

Finally we are resting. Moonlight plays about the door, but it does not light the corners of our new prison, where I imagine smallpox has become a great, hairy creature ready to creep across the rough boards toward my sleeping family.

When I am sure that Mother is asleep, I rise, get the one lighted candle the British left on a shelf near the back wall, and place it so that I can see the sleeping little ones. We have no netting, and two fat mosquitoes hover over little Sarah's face. Asleep she looks even younger than her five years. Gently, I brush back the golden hair from her round cheek. Suddenly, I fear that I might burst with the almost unbearable need to protect her, and I know that what I am about to do is right, no matter the consequence to me. I take the candle and move toward the door, hoping a British sentry does not see the moving light and come rushing in to see what I am up to. To my relief there is no sudden intrusion.

At the doorway, I lean for a moment against the frame, gathering my courage. Not wanting to stare at the stockade, I turn my eyes up to the moon. It is full, a bright ball so close that I think I could toss a pebble smack into its middle.

I know, of course, that there is but one moon. Do the rays, then, which bathe us in silver, belong to Carolina or to the British who now possess our land?

Euven, no doubt, would say it is because there is but one moon, one earth, one God, that we men must learn to live in peace. "Euven's little brother and sisters are not being exposed to smallpox," I whisper to the moon. The moon does not reply.

In order to give my family a needed rest, I have decided to wait until just before dawn to carry out my plan. Perhaps I will sleep just a wink or two myself. I slide down to the floor, and with my legs spread across the doorway, I finally float off into slumber.

I wake just as a bright spot appears over the roof of our ballroom, which is now filled with British soldiers asleep on cots.

I remember how the smell of their burning tobacco alarmed my mother. "It will be only by God's mercy," she said to me one night, "if some worn soldier does not fall asleep with his pipe and set fire to us all."

I smile and think that it may be by God's mercy

that I have had this idea, and I know I will need his mercy to carry it out. First I spread my blanket near the door. Neither Sarah nor baby Rebecca stir when I move them to the blanket beside the door. George is harder for me to lift, and he moans as I strain to rise with him. I freeze, certain that my mother will wake, but perhaps because of her day spent scrubbing the cabin she does not.

There is no way to move Mary without waking Mother, so when George is settled beside the two smaller ones, I am ready. After assuring myself that Mother remains asleep, I take the candle and the blanket upon which George slept to the back corner of the cabin.

I hold my breath for the moment it takes the twisted blanket to light. First there is a thin thread of smoke. Then in an instant a bright flame reaches toward the sacking tacked to the cabin wall. I struggle with the impulse to smother the flickering red spot as it touches the sacking, but a fitful cry comes from George as he turns against the hard floor. I remember that I am doing this thing for my little brother and sisters.

I watch as the flame climbs quickly up the sacking. A cracking sound begins to fill the cabin, and at the exact moment, when it is too late to dash the fire with the water bucket, I scream to my mother.

When we are outside, we stand shaking for a moment, and I can see the shock of this awakening in the little one's eyes. We stare at the flames.

I am still shaking, but it is not from the cold. I have small hope that the British will see the fire as an accident. Of course I will not let them blame my mother.

What will they do to me? I shrug my shoulders. There will be no place for my family here now. Surely, my mother and the others will be sent to Burndale. They will not be exposed to smallpox there, and there will not be so many British soldiers.

My mother turns to me. There is no doubt that she knows what I have done. "Joey, how did you start the fire?" she asks.

"The candle and a blanket." I am quick to add, "But there was no danger. I moved them first." With my hand I indicate the smaller children. I wait for my mother's response, and I notice the sun has changed from a ball of orange to bright yellow.

Mother shifts Rebecca to her other arm, puts the free one around my shoulders, and leans her head down to rest against mine. "I am afraid," she whispers. "They won't just let us get by with this."

Almost before the words are out of her mouth an officer comes to us. "You did this on purpose, madam," he says, and I half expect him to draw his sword and run my mother through.

"No!" I step out toward the soldier. With a little cry of protest, Mother reaches toward me, but I pay her no mind. "My mother had nothing to do with the fire, sir," I say. "It is I who put the candle to the blanket while she slept."

And so I am now in chains in the keeping room. I was dragged into the house by an officer, and was taken to Lord Rawdon himself. He is a young man, yet his eyes are hard, and he holds his head in the most arrogant way.

He watched me as I walked toward him between my two guards. There was a cruel twist to his smile, and I thought that he would surely kill me. "Bit of a scrapper, aren't you, boy?" It seemed there was a trace of admiration in his voice, and I began to have hope of being spared.

"Yes," I said, and my gaze met his straight on.

"No more! We can't have it. I've no time for childish warfare. There are armies for us to fight. A few days in chains may quiet you." He nodded his head with satisfaction and waved dismissal. Then as we turned to leave he added, "After that you can serve our men. Make a little slave of you, we will."

It does not matter. Just as I hoped, my family is being sent to Burndale. I am not allowed to say goodbye to my mother, but my spunky little sister sneaks down the keeping room stairs to see me. A guard is on duty at the large front doors, but he seems unaware that I am to see no family.

We have had little to say to each other of late, and for a moment there is an awkward silence between us. "It was brave, what you did," Mary says.

I smile, glad to be at last her hero. "There's not much time. I hate to leave you behind." She reaches for my hand. "Please don't be mad at me, Joey."

I shrug. "I am not mad now." I am sorry I yelled at her. "You'll have Uncle Samuel to make you laugh." Mother's younger brother is a great favorite of Mary's and of mine. I am proud of the fact that he was the first white person to be born in Camden and even more of the fact that despite his Quaker upbringing he went off to Charleston to fight the British.

Mary tries to smile. My eyes fall on the books that stand on a small shelf near the table where Euven and I do lessons. Suddenly an idea comes to me, and before I can change my mind I say, "Take some books, Mary, as many as you can carry. You can study them, and when we are together again we will talk about what you have learned."

"Your books?" She seems to doubt her ears.

"Yes. It's high time you had some real learning. I'd help you carry them if I could." I hold up my chained hands.

"You know Father does not believe a woman should concern herself with much knowledge from books." Her brow is drawn tight, and she watches my face closely.

"Father may not always be right." The words come out without my having planned them, and they seem to bounce from brick wall to brick wall. Mary and I stare at each other. Each of us knows that an important moment in my life is occurring.

"Won't you need these?" She is already across the room and gathering books from the shelf.

"If ever Euven is allowed to come again, he will bring more. Hurry, Mary."

When her arms are full, she goes as quickly as she can toward the stairs. Then turning back, she comes to place a quick kiss upon my cheek. At the moment I can no longer see her form in the doorway, a loneliness deeper than any I have ever felt comes over me.

Lord Rawdon is true to his word. I spend three days in heavy chains that cut into my feet and hands. Cato smears a thick yellow salve on my wounds, and he brings me a mat like his to spread upon the floor at night.

On the first night I lie awake for many hours. I think Cato is sleeping, but he speaks into the darkness that surrounds us. "Misery eases some, boy. I sure understands misery. Every day since they brings me away from Africa. You knows something, boy? I done lost every soul I loves. My mammy, sold. My wife, sold. Three little childs, sold. All gone, jus' gone. Oh, I knows misery."

He does not seem to expect a reply, and I can think of nothing to say. Down toward the creek an owl hoots into the night. I hear no sounds from the soldiers inside the house or from those in either army who sleep outside.

For a time I try to pretend that no war wages. I tell myself that my father and mother and the children are all asleep upstairs. I say that Cato and I have decided to sleep here in the keeping room as a sort of lark, and that he has fallen asleep telling me the stories of his early, happy life in Africa.

Then I give up efforts to create a make-believe world. A war is not easily pretended away.

Chapter Nine

Dear Father,

I live now in the keeping room, sleeping on a mat near Cato. I wonder about your life in prison. Even if we win this war, even if you come home and we take down the fence around our house, we will never be the same. The boot scars will be always in our floors. The changes will be always in our hearts.

On the third day, after the chains are removed, I am put to work. It is the prisoners for whom I do most of my jobs, carrying food, tending to the sick, cleaning the filthy pen where they are caged. My body aches for rest, but my spirit is strangely at peace. Rawdon thinks to punish me. Yet for the first time since this terrible war began, I feel calm.

I am often outside now, and it is good to see the sky. Summer is gone. October breezes sweep rusty red needles from the pine trees. By winter their color will change again to a grayish brown, and thick carpets of them will cover the front garden where the burial ditches are. Still I will know the graves are there.

One evening when it is almost dusk, Captain Keegan calls me to follow him. I have just carried fresh water to thirsty men, and I am leaning for a second against the stockade fence to rest my weary body.

"This way with you," shouts Keegan, and I trot to follow him through the keeping room door. There he points to a shelf where military supplies rest. "Take the rag," he says, "and the boot black. My boots want shining."

I think of the boy, Andy Jackson, who refused to do this very same task. I long to refuse and think that I too could endure a cut on the cheek or on the hand. However, I feel certain that if Captain Keegan takes a sword to me, it will be my heart or liver that bears the slash.

I want to live. At the moment I want most to live because I can see the woodbox. Biddy is gone, allowed to go with my mother because the military cook did not want her in the kitchen. Still I fill the woodbox, and still I dream of using the pistol. Head down, I fetch the needed materials, then bend to shine the Captain's boots.

A small green worm crawls across the floor. Just before I put my rag to the left boot, the Captain lifts that foot and squashes the worm against the brick floor. In this man's eyes, I am worth little more than the worm.

When nighttime at last brings rest, I lie again on the mat beside Cato's. My body aches and my eyes are heavy. Cato is restless. He turns and turns. Then he rises. I can see him in the moonlight that comes through the windows. He sits against a brick wall, and he wipes with a cloth at a small white stone. He begins to hum. Occasionally there is a word or two. His voice is soft, and I cannot make out the words. I think they are strange, a language I do not know.

I am tired, but too interested to sleep. Sitting up, I listen and wonder if Cato would stop singing if I move closer. I stay on my mat, but I speak. "Is it an African song?"

Cato nods. "'Fore they tore me way. 'Fore my misery days. Mostly the words is gone from my ol' mind. It be a song 'bout a river. That much I knows."

"How old were you, Cato?"

"Five, just five years old, holding my mammy's hand. My pa, he fight. They splits his head open."

I am horrified, but I do not want him to stop talking. "Is the stone from Africa?"

Cato laughs. "This be a rock I just finds down by

the mill last year. Ain't got nothing from that life, not one thing but bits of that ol' song. I 'member the river some and big birds flying, not my mammy's face, just my pa's head. Fifty years I lives a slave life."

He starts to hum again, but this time there are no words. I am filled with sadness. It comes to me to tell Cato what my mother has said about his freedom. I will promise that when this war is over, he will be no longer a slave. I start to open my mouth, but I do not. Suddenly, I fear his anger.

I imagine that I am a boy younger than George, that my father is killed, that I am ripped away from my part of Carolina, so that the Wateree River becomes only a dim memory. I imagine that then I am forced away from my mother and that later I lose my wife and children as Cato did. For fifty years I own little more than a stone that is truly my own. I imagine that when I am old and tired, some little boy waves a hope of freedom at me. I think that I would shout, "Too late!" I decide to say nothing.

"You gets yo'self some sleeping now," Cato tells me.

I lie back down. "I will never hold slaves," I say to the man across the room.

"That be good," he answers. "That sure be a good way, young master."

"No. I want never to be called master." There in the dark I see suddenly my father's face. I who am my father's son find myself with ideas that oppose his. I have encouraged my sister to study. I have promised never to hold slaves. Am I betraying my father? The thought unnerves me, but I am far too weary to deal with it. I fall asleep before Cato comes back to his mat.

Chapter Ten

Dear Father,

It is my birthday, but no one here knows or cares. I think of the merriment of last year, and of the feast we had, sweet potatoes, catfish stew, turkey, rice, peach leather, and lots of syllabub. It seems long ago. I am so much older now, but not because I am thirteen.

I wish Euven would come again to see me. The prisoners, whom I tend with almost no help from the British, are kind to me. There are those among them who at one time would have made good choices for shared conversations and laughter. But I've no desire to make a friend of a man who tomorrow may be hanged while I am forced to watch.

New American prisoners are frequently brought

here from nearby battles, and the hangings continue to be held regularly. Captain Harkins, I know, tries somewhat to spare me. The captain is often in his quarters upstairs at such a time, and when possible he arranges for me to help him copy reports or sweep the floor.

Once during such a time he told me of an injury he suffered when he was in Massachusetts, early on in the war. "My leg was badly hurt. Unable to walk, I fell among the other wounded and the dead. The battle was over, but still no one came to help me. The sun beat down on me, and I lay drifting in and out of consciousness. I woke to see a form bending over me and holding out a canteen. He straightened my wounded leg, which twisted when I fell, and he gave me a drink of water. He was an American soldier going about to ease suffering among the British."

"He did a thing I would never have done," I say, and I begin again to sweep at the floor.

Captain Harkins is at his desk. For a second I think he has not heard me, but then he looks up from his papers. "By my word, Joseph, I wish you did not hate me so."

I swipe at the floor with a mighty energy, an energy born of the hate Captain Harkins would have me give up. I could not, even if I wanted, give up that hate. What then would keep me alive? My thoughts are filled with little else than the gun at the bottom of the keep-

ing room woodbox. I will hold that gun, and I will kill
a redcoat. Only when I have done so will peace come
to me.

When I walked this morning to the prison pen,
there was a crunchy sound from the heavy frost beneath
my feet. A group of birds are black against the bright
sky. They seem late in their departure for a warmer
climate. I wish the men who huddle in the rude huts
before me could go with those birds.

Food grows more and more scarce. Our little com-
munity could never feed so many. The British still eat
well, but the prisoners in their makeshift huts have little
more than watery soup.

Out at Burndale it is the same. I imagine little
George and Sarah with thin faces. Even small Rebecca,
I fear, has lost her baby roundness. I am never allowed
to leave these grounds, but Cato is not watched so
closely. At night he sometimes hunts by torch light for
wild pigeons in the swamp and carries his bounty to my
mother before dawn.

He comes back, muddy, cold, and exhausted after I
have had my meager bowl of breakfast porridge. I worry
about Cato's health. He no longer wears the bright
clothes that were the uniform of the principal house
slave. "These suits me better," he says of the rough
clothing he now wears. I marvel how I never thought
that Cato's uniform made him look like a fancy doll,

but I fret because his frame grows thinner and more bent beneath his coarse shirt.

I wonder too what has become of my waistcoat and linen shirts. I am only curious. Like Cato I feel better in my work clothes, and I notice that my britches are shorter than they were when first I put them on. I am thinner, but taller. The British cannot stop my growth.

My mother sends me a note. "Joey," she writes, "we think of you always. I am allowed now to send your father letters and to receive his. He is well. I know it would bring him pleasure to have word from you. Cato can bring your letter when he comes next. I have had word too from your brothers. One day we will all be together again. My darling son, I pray for your safety and that your eyes are on the inward light."

After I have read the note, I sit for a long time beside the keeping room fire. I think of my brothers. They have experienced nothing of this war. How can they ever understand?

I go to a shelf where there is paper and pen. If no redcoat calls me to work, I will write a letter to my father, a real letter, one that will be posted. I settle at the table and am undisturbed for some time. Yet my page remains blank. My eyes go to the woodbox, and I put the pen away. Perhaps I will not write to my father until I have made my big strike against the British. Then I will have something to say.

Each night Cato and I place our mats as close as possible to the big hearth. We have but one blanket and share it, both of us glad to have also the heat of another body near. One night before we sleep, I tell him about my father's gun. "It is there still, waiting." I sit up so that I can see the box. "One day my chance will come, and I will kill a redcoat. At least one of the hated soldiers will die because of me."

Cato's response from his mat beside me is a surprise. "Don't yo' do it, Mister Joey. Don't yo' go and do no such thing. I kills me a man, needed killing too, but them eyes they follows me. They watches me while I lives."

"But doubtless he was not as evil as these redcoats," I argue.

"Most these men, they just soldiers. They got bad jobs, that's all. War be like that, I reckon." Cato closes his eyes. His now familiar snoring tells me any argument I might voice would be wasted.

A few days before Christmas a snow begins to fall, and a wonderful thing happens. Euven is allowed to come for a visit. He has with him a small basket of tea cakes. "Hannah made them for me, and I want to share them with thee." He places the basket on the keeping room table.

"You should keep them for yourself," I say, but my

eyes do not leave the cakes. Cato has showed me how to make a kind of tea from the dried leaves of a blackberry vine. He keeps a tin of the leaves in the small box where we have our few personal things.

First I wrap two of the cakes in a cloth and put them away for Cato. Then I make cups of tea for Euven and me. It is a celebration. I am smiling, and the expression feels strange upon my face. "If only I could have lessons again," I say.

He laughs. "So thee misses geometry?"

"Just history and literature. I let Mary take my books. She wants so to learn."

"What pleasure it would give me to have Mary for a pupil." He turns his head westward and with the broad-brim hat in his hand he makes a sweeping wave in that direction. "When I am out there, I will endeavor to gather all manner of young ones to me, boys, girls, the Negro children, and the young ones we call Indian, to whom this land truly belongs."

I shake my head. "You have strange ideas, Euven Wylie. Even for a Quaker, you have daft ideas."

He slaps at me with his hat. For a time we scuffle playfully as if there is no war. Then I hear an officer call out, "Order arms." A group of soldiers is standing inspection before the big keeping room doors, and I hope the drill will last long enough for Euven and me to have our tea in peace. I want to hear about Hannah and about the special pine chest Euven is carving for her as a Christmas gift.

We have each eaten one cake when our merrymaking is interrupted with, "What are you doing there, Quaker man?" I look up to see Watkins, the man who slapped me on the porch, and I know the good time is over. My fingers tighten around my cup.

"I have news that just might interest you, Mr. Quaker." Watkins is smiling, but there is an evil look in his eyes. The air is thick with trouble. My heart beats fast, but Euven's face shows no disturbance. I long to see him rise up.

If only Watkins did not have the musket in his hand, Euven could best him easily. Watkins is nothing but blubber. How good it would be to see Euven take him on.

Watkins comes toward the table. "I just got word that me and two others will be moving into the Goodnight house. You're acquainted with the folks there, ain't you, Mr. Quaker fellow?"

The British soldiers are being billeted in homes of people all over town, who, like us, have no choice but to take them in. A frown begins about Euven's lips, but it never quite forms. "Thee will find Mistress Goodnight to be a fine cook," he says.

Watkins laughs. "And I'll wager I find the young Miss Goodnight real warm on a cold evening."

Suddenly Euven is up. The table shakes as he pushes away, but his voice is calm. "I must ask thee not to speak Miss Goodnight's name so."

Watkins laughs. "Keep your breath to cool your porridge." He turns to walk away.

"Wait." Euven's face is red now. Watkins is near the stairs. Euven takes a step to follow. Suddenly Watkins whirls, and the butt of the musket strikes Euven's face. There is a cry of pain. He reels, his arms flailing the air. I do not wait to see him fall.

I am up, but I do not rush to my injured friend. In one second I am on my knees beside the woodbox and have emptied it. The pistol is cold to my hand, but the blood rushing through my body feels hot. I am about to use my father's gun to put a hole in a hated redcoat.

Euven does not stir, and a trickle of blood runs from his forehead to the stone floor. My hand is shaking as I level the gun.

I hesitate one moment too long. Watkins is grinning, and his musket is pointed directly at me. "I'll rid the regiment of one pesky rebel brat and do it proper like by way of self-defense."

There is a blur of movement by the stairs, and a red-sleeved arm lunges toward Watkins's gun. A great explosion rattles the tin cups on the table. I look down, expecting to find a dark red stain beginning to spread across my shirt.

I have not been hit. Confused, I look again at Watkins and am surprised to see the confusion on my face mirrored in his. I follow his gaze to the floor. The spreading red stain that should have been my blood is there. I see with horror that the blood belongs to Captain Harkins.

There are other soldiers now, coming down the stairs and through the big keeping room doors. They bend over the fallen captain. The gun is taken from Watkins's hands, and he is marched away at gunpoint. Someone has gone to Euven, and he is helped to sit up. I want to go to him, but my feet will not move. I watch what goes on in the room, but I do not feel as if I am really there.

"He's dead," says one of the soldiers who examines Captain Harkins. "No doubt about it, war's over for this man."

Chapter Eleven

I no longer write imaginary letters to my father. Someday I will write a real letter, but I do not yet know what words I will use.

Euven arranged for Captain Harkins to be buried in the Quaker cemetery, and I am surprised that he was able to secure permission for me to attend the burial. The Quakers do not believe in decorated graves, but on a small stone Euven chisels, "Matthew Harkins of Dover, England. He was a friend." There is no mention of his military rank or of the war.

Captain Harkins was well liked. Many British soldiers stand about. There are drum rolls as the burial takes place, but I do not think of the redcoats or of the music. My mind is full of the captain's son, a baby who will never see his father because of me.

The snow is still falling and will soon be deep. We do not often have big snows. I watch the fat flakes falling across the graves, and words come to my memory. They are from the play Euven and I read: "It is the dead, not the living, who make the longest demands."

When it is over, Euven and I must separate. His head is swollen, but he pats my shoulder. "Don't trouble yourself over my wound," he says. "It will heal."

I move with the British back to my keeping room, and I think that, like the eyes that follow Cato, I will see those blue eyes of Captain Harkins always.

The winter passes slowly. Once Cato is able to steal a cow from the scrawny herd the British secure somewhere. He hides the animal in the forest and by night drives it to Burndale. Biddy will cook it over an open fire in the swamp and sneak meat to my family.

Euven is not allowed to visit me again, but Cato brings word that he is married now and has taken Hannah and her mother to his small home. I am pleased.

On a day in late March, I am sweeping the upstairs veranda when I spot the blue-violet wildflowers that have sprung up in the clearing just at the edge of the woods. I stop my work, walk to the railing, and stare. I marvel that spring has actually returned to South Carolina. Soon the honeysuckle will blossom once more around the gallows in the side garden. Will this war go on, as I, a prisoner, mark the beginning of spring after spring?

There is as yet no new growth in the vegetable gardens. Even the British are now hungry. "It may be de empty bellies that beats 'em," Cato tells me one night, and I, having observed Cato's wisdom, begin to hope.

On the 25th of April there is a battle just outside Camden at Hobkirk Hill. Lord Rawdon and his troops return claiming victory, but even I can see that the army is weakened. Moreover, the slight triumph is meaningless. American troops, driven back but a few miles, still surround Camden except for a narrow passage leading in the direction of Charleston. I stand, when I can, on the veranda, stare toward the coast, and imagine the British marching away from Camden. I can almost smile.

It begins on a morning in early May. Cato wakes me before dawn. "They going," he says. "You got to hide yo'self away." But it is too late. A British soldier is beside us and orders us to the ballroom to gather blankets thrown on the floor by soldiers in a hurry. From beneath us there is the sound of wood being struck with axes. When I can slip away, I go at once to the dining room, and I stand in the doorway, watching.

Two soldiers are swinging axes, chopping at my mother's mahogany table. I am unable to turn away until nothing is left except pieces that one man begins to heave through the glass panes of the back window. His companion now starts to hack at the sideboard.

Everywhere it is the same, broken beds, shattered mirrors. Bayonets have torn at the flowers on the sofa, and stuffing tumbles out to cover the shredded damask. What is left of Mother's Sea Leaf china is smashed against the now scarred floors of our once fine home.

Rage leaves me weak. Why must they destroy what is left behind? From the upstairs window I see fires all about town, and know that destruction does not touch only Kershaw House.

Likely they will burn this house too, though I wonder if they would take time to break so much if they planned for it all to go up in flames. Will they leave behind, unharmed, the son of Colonel Joseph Kershaw? I find the possibility not a strong one.

Am I, who have survived these long and terrible eleven months with the British, to die on this their last day? Weak from lack of food and from the horror of many days, at first the thought of death does not disturb me overmuch. But gradually I begin to think of Mother, Mary, and the little ones. What agony for them to come back home to find my body among the ruins of home.

I gather my strength and begin to walk, staying close to the wall. Cato and I have been separated, but he comes to find me in the keeping room. "They 'pears to forget 'bout us," he says. "We got to slip out 'fore they burns this house."

Cato goes to a back window. I look around once at my keeping room before I follow. Outside I stare at the stockade.

Many of the prisoners have been loaded into wagons and driven away by the British. I wonder if those too weak to move have been left behind, but Cato pulls me away from the pen toward the woods.

When we reach the cover of trees, I stop. "Come on," urges Cato, but I do not move.

"You go," I say, and I lean against a pine. "I want to stay here. I want to see what happens to Kershaw House."

Cato stays beside me. We watch the last British soldier leave our house and green. The somber sounds of the English drums and fife do not completely disappear before lighter notes begin to mix. "Our men," I shout. "Our men are coming!" I am running from the woods and stumble over a fallen dead limb. Rising, I notice that to my left are two dogwood trees, full of white and wonderful blossoms. "The dogwoods are in bloom!" I shout.

I do not stop. I run past the house and down the green. I run, and jump, and shout. The Wateree River calls to me. It is spring, and I long to dash to the water's edge, to see a white heron rise up in flight before me.

But I look back toward the house. Some of our troops will be left to care for sick prisoners. I want to see what is happening, and the redcoats, I am sure, have left Burndale also. Soon my uncle will bring my mother and the children. They will be eager to make sure that I have not been injured or killed.

The river will have to wait. I pick up a small tree branch. Dragging it through the sand and grass behind me as I did when I was a child, I turn back. I will sit on the front steps of Kershaw House, and I will strain for the first sight of my family returning home.

When at last they come, it is not in my uncle's fine carriage, which I suppose has been taken by the British. Instead an old wagon, pulled by one thin horse, comes up the hill. I do not run toward them. Instead I hurry inside to watch from the doorway.

I want to look at each one. Uncle Samuel helps Mother down. She is thin, but still straight. Mary jumps to the ground at once and is running. George and Sarah have grown tall, and little Rebecca's steps are no longer the uncertain ones of a baby.

Mother sees me and holds out her arms. "Welcome home," I shout. "Welcome home to Kershaw House."

Chapter Twelve

Dear Son,

My captors are allowing me to write a brief note to each of you. My prison is damp and uncomfortable. I pass the days thinking of South Carolina and of my dear family. By the time this reaches you it will be spring, and the air will be filled with the yellow pollen from Camden's guardians, the pine trees. How I long to supervise the spring planting, walking with you by my side. We get no real news here, but whispered rumor says that the British are suffering great losses. I pray such is the truth and that I will be home shortly. I remain always

Your loving father,
Joseph Kershaw

★ The British have been gone now for a fortnight. My mother does not complain about the condition of our home. She has had a banister made for the inside stairs.

People say that the rumors Father hears are true. The war is winding down. It is time for me to write him a letter.

On a day in late May, I go out to the veranda. There is a small table there. I take a quill and paper. Mary has found flower seeds, which she plants now in the front garden. Soon green vines will push through the scarred soil, and bright buds will cover the burial ditches.

I sit at the table. For a few minutes I stare at the blank paper, but once I have written, "Dear Father," other words begin to come quickly to my mind.

The British are gone from Camden. You will come home soon, and we will be here waiting. There are some things I must tell you. For one thing, Mother has given Cato and Biddy both their freedom and land. She has bought Biddy's husband too and given him his free papers. I think you will agree that it was right for her to do so. Without them we should not have survived our ordeal.

I have given Mary my books. Our Mary is determined to have an education, and I hope you will decide to provide her one as good as any boy's. Mary is brave and strong, and I believe we will all be proud of her.

But the greatest change of all, I think, is in me. I can take no joy, ever again, in any battle. A British officer died here to save my life. Captain Harkins was a just man whose death does not allow me to hate a man only because he fights on the other side.

There is also the matter of slavery. Having learned what it is to be a prisoner, I can never imprison another human being by making him my slave.

I have no wish to distress you, Father, but I am not at all sure you will want me to manage your holdings in the future. Such a task would be a great honor, but I am not the boy I was before this war.

Often, I have stood on the veranda of Kershaw House and watched. I will be there watching for you, and I hope you will be glad to see me, the son who has changed but who loves and respects you still.

Joseph Kershaw Jr.

After I walk to town to post my letter, I go back to the keeping room. Mother protests because I still sleep on a mat spread upon this brick floor. Perhaps someday I can return to the room upstairs where I slept as a boy. For now the keeping room seems right.

$15.95

DATE			